To Jer[...]

Who is[...]

Lov[...]

Dot

CW00417522

Simple Stories About Women

Twelve Tales by
Dorothy Schwarz

First Published 1998 by IRON Press
5, Marden Terrace, Cullercoats,
North Shields, Northumberland NE30 4PD, UK
Tel/Fax: (0191) 253 1901

Typeset by David Stephenson
in Elan 10 point

Printed by Peterson Printers
South Shields

Some of these stories were previously published
in *IRON, Panurge, Tees Valley Writer* and *Raconteur,*
and broadcast on *BBC Radio 4*

Cover design by Michael J. Adam
Book design by Peter Mortimer

ISBN 0-906228-0-68-9

FIRST EDITION

IRON Press books are represented by:
Signature Book Representation
Sun House, 2 Little Peter Street
Manchester M15 4PS
Tel: (0161) 834 8767
Fax: (0161) 834 8656
e-mail: signatur@dircon.co.uk

northern
arts
PROMOTING THE ARTS
IN THE NORTH

Simple Stories about Women

Too Much Salt   5

In Our Tribe the Women are not Shepherds   18

Duet for Three Voices   24

Playing the Game   31

Separate and Together   52

The Sound of Silence   57

Lottie's Little Habit   75

The Matriarch   82

Riding Round Eros   90

Virtual Reality   89

What Big Eyes, Grandma?   105

Love in the Time of...   112

Photograph - Walter Schwarz

DOROTHY SCHWARZ was born and educated in London, and has spent almost thirty years travelling and living with her journalist husband Walter in Israel, India, Nigeria and France and other places which provide the locations for many of her stories.

Settled in Colchester since 1984, she teaches Creative Writing at the local Adult Education Institute.Since her five children have left, or are leaving the nest, she finds more and more time for writing and believes that the short story is one of the finest genres through which to learn the craft of writing.

She is interested in ecology, German Shepherd dogs , literature, her family and horses, not necessarily in that order. Widely published in the small presses and broadcast on radio, this is her first published short story collection.Later in 1998 she and Walter will have published their joint book *Living Lightly - Travels in Post Consumer Society* (Jon Carpenter).

Too
Much
Salt

Occasionally, I dream of him. No longer a little boy the way I last saw him but an immense, bulky, black figure – standing against the cottage window – blocking out the light.

When Elijah entered our lives, Alex was barely six and I was teaching at the local Adult Education Centre in our market town.

I teach Philosophy (Parts One and Two.) Don't laugh. It does seem a bit funny – me – teaching philosophy. But I'd studied it. Seemed a good choice at the time. Grammar school girl, scholarship to Oxford, Dad ever so proud, Grandma couldn't see the point. 'Like you'll be married – then what's all the learning worth?'

She never did see the point. Died during my first year. If I hadn't read philosophy, I wouldn't have met Robert. Drawn together in the college French club because both of us too shy to help ourselves to the nouvelle Beaujolais at the end of the table. Since then, we've organised a peaceful, orderly life that I'm proud of. I don't know why people knock ordinary life nowadays.

I should've finished the degree but Louise was well on the way and so I didn't. My folks were very good about that. Robert's not so. A hedge grew all the way round their property and I thought the frayed carpets on the walls were put up against the damp until Robert's Mum, Margery, informed me they were tapestries.

Margery tried to look down on me. She couldn't; I'm half-a-head taller. I guess she didn't like Jews. Went a bit red when she learnt that Dad's surname Curzon was Anglicised from Kurtsman. Dad was lucky to get out – none of his folks did. So you see I have a built in – you might say genetic – predisposition towards tolerance.

And you need tolerance – in my life. Take a student like Alice, overweight and contradictory; she can wear you down, exhaust your goodwill, erode your confidence.

Alice de Groote fancied herself an undiscovered writer. Don't we all? She'd written her memoirs: South Africa – the sixties under Apartheid. She'd sit with her fat knees spread wide apart, glimpse of pink bloomers, her grey head bobbing up and down and read excerpts. A dreadful style and as for the contents – if she'd done one tenth of the things she claimed – the secret police would've locked her up.

'They are su-u-ch lovely, lovely people. I am proud to have played my part!' Alice's ringing tones made several people in the pub raise their heads.

Since the ANC didn't need her after Independence, so she said, and who can blame them, she'd become involved with Somalia. Such wonderful people, such wonderful, wonderful people. Did I know that the Queen of Sheba came from there? No, I didn't. Didn't I want to get involved? No, I didn't.

'I suppose with your background, Zionism appeals more?'

I blushed. Ridiculous how those sort of remarks aggravate – even made by Alice.

"Spose I could be interested in Somalia... ?'

Alice fiddled with a straggling grey hair on her moustache. 'Oh, wouldn't interest you... children of your own... too busy.'

' No, I'm not – not particularly. Louise is away at uni. There's only Alex.'

Alice twitched out the hair, examined it and launched into another fabulous tale involving a Somali princess, in exile to England after her husband's assassination, now eking out a miserable living in London while her eight year-old son went to boarding school. On later reflection, it struck me if the mother eked a miserable living – who paid the fees?

'In a manner of speaking, I'm a sort of, a sort of, say, guardian to this child,' said Alice. Her glasses misted over. She wiped them. 'A child who has suffered... But then how could you know of such things...?'

Two can play at that game. I lit a cigarette.

'Now this boy, this suffering child... Should I tell you the whole story?'

I inhaled deeply and blew three smoke rings; they wafted up to the ceiling. Alice began pulling at her moustache again. I relented. She so much wanted to be pressed.

'Yes, you should, please.'

'His name is Elijah.'

'What like the prophet?'

'Not really – Anglicisation of his Somali name. All the suffering...' a big sigh, 'has affected his little mind.'

'Poor little chap. What a tragedy!'

Just a phrase, meaningless enough, to hurry her along. No way. Once she had my attention, Alice was holding on.

'Another gin and tonic?'

I shook my head, stubbed out my cigarette: 'I really have to be going.'

Firmness pays off. Alice stopped procrastinating; the complicated tale involved sex, espionage, money, and child psychology. What interested me was the child himself.

'He's totally out of control. He has gone through six foster homes and three schools.'

'Why doesn't he live with his mother?'

'Part of the unhingement,' said Alice. 'He claims... Oh, well, you don't want to hear all this. She is a real princess.'

I don't know where Alice got the idea that princesses were incapable of bad behaviour (perhaps she never read the papers.)

'Finding a new foster home, I'm at my wit's ends.'

I murmured she didn't have far to go.

'What's that?'

Nothing.'

'Just can't have him with me, simply can't cope.'

Alice! An admission like that from Alice, who didn't balk at Wittgenstein and considered herself the equal of Heidigger and would arrive at our end-of-term get-togethers insisting (and succeeding) that we drank her home-made dandelion wine.

'It's weekends. Exeats from his boarding school. He needs somewhere to go. My place no good at all. He's allergic to cats. (Alice had seven.) It wouldn't do for you either. You are too busy and besides, you're not used to black people, are you?'

How dare she patronise me like that! She baited her trap – in I fell.

I agreed to fetch Elijah from his school on Saturday afternoon, take him home for tea and if, in Alice's phrase, 'You get along famously,' we would offer to stand in as temporary foster parents. Once she had my agreement, Alice said solemnly; 'I must warn you that the child is off the rails.'

The prep school, Gothic red brick and turrets, nestled behind a screen of copper beeches. The Waiting Room had today's *Times* and this month's *Country Life*. The Housemaster handing over Elijah wore an all-purpose smile and Varsity tie. Elijah wore wide-legged grey shorts, school tie and too-small cap. Even in that ridiculous outfit he was gorgeous – like a Greek statue, his nose and forehead a straight line, his eyelashes sweeping his cheeks. Oh, my dear, dumpy Alex! What a contrast!

In spite of voting Labour all our married lives, I couldn't help being a tiny bit impressed with Elijah. You see, I'd never met a Prince before. Then Elijah held out a shapely, long-fingered hand and opened his mouth: 'Allo, Missis. 'Ow are yer?'

The Housemaster kept the smile going: 'Elijah has attended several London schools previously.' He shepherded us to my station wagon. 'Now do have a simply splendid day – sure that you will.'

The 'completely impossible' boy did up his seat belt without being asked and flashed that incredible smile again. Within minutes we were chatting away – inconsequential stuff – Alice had exaggerated as usual. Then he made his first unsettling remark.

'Don't expect yer'll keep me fer long,' Elijah said.'They never does.' His long lashes glistened.

Elijah and Alex sniffed around one another – stiff-legged like two strange dogs, Alex only two years younger, a little unformed boy. I left them kicking a football. Alex isn't exactly backward but he is a bit – maybe you'd call it – shy.

Robert grumbled: why should we foster another child when we had one of our own still at home, the cat and his old Mother to visit?

'Margery doesn't need us. Elijah does.'

The two boys came in for hot, buttered crumpets. Alex said with great excitement: 'Elijah's bin teaching me how to catapult.'

Oh, dear! Robert put on his schoolmaster's face and held out his hand, palm-up.

Elijah handed over a home-made catapult. 'Yer can git sparrers wiv it.'

'No, Elijah. We do not 'git' sparrows with anything.'

'Ok, yer the boss.'

Elijah's next exploit was to encourage Alex to climb the cherry tree. I looked out the kitchen window and saw both boys whooping at the top. 'Get down,' I yelled, fingers crossed. Elijah showed Alex the right toe holds. They climbed down with no mishaps. I must stop being an over-cautious Mum. And taking Elijah to Sainsburys, I enjoyed the effect his looks caused. He had charming manners and held open the car door and carried the plastic shopping bags without being asked. Even Robert was mollified when Elijah asked for chess lessons. Alex had never shown the least interest.

That night Alex wet his bed.

'You're paying too much attention to Elijah,' I warned.

'Pop psychology never Freud any onions.'

'Robert, I'm serious.'

'So am I.' Robert included Elijah in his nightly prayers with Alex. Robert has special non-denominational ones the RE teacher at his school uses. Elijah said: 'Ain't never 'ad prayers in a 'ouse before. I like 'em.'

Half-an-hour before we were due to drive back to Suffolk, Elijah poked round the garden with a torch. I couldn't imagine what he was up to until he came inside, having picked every single crocus in the garden, squashed the flowerheads in a ruff of silver foil and said, 'Wish I could stay 'ere.'

Hugging him, he felt hard in my arms – not child-like at all. So far not a mention of his Mother. Robert could laugh all he wanted to about pop-psychology but I knew I was handling him right. He'd tell us what we needed to know in his own time. Those tales of Alice's – pure exaggeration.

When I drove him back to school, Alex wanted to come too. The two boys sat in the back and giggled. I handed Elijah over to the Housemaster and said: 'He's behaved beautifully.' The Housemaster nodded.

Alice sounded genuinely delighted. Maybe I'd been misjudging her. 'That's just what the boy needs. Something stable. A good family atmosphere. Well done, Sara.' I couldn't help a slight smirk.

The logical next step seemed to be to invite Elijah for the Easter holidays. We are extraordinarily lucky to have the use of a tiny stone cottage which Margery and Alfred had bought years ago. We would leave our nice four-bedroomed house, ten minutes from the Town

Centre, pile everything, except the cat, into the station wagon and in five hours be driving up the mountain road into a countryside full of astonishing surprises – hillsides littered with heaps of sharp-edged grey slate from disused quarries with ferns and heather growing everywhere. Waterfalls leap down from the rocks and sheep, agile as goats leap up the rocks. The valley is magic (I don't exaggerate); if a sleeping dragon awoke from under the tumulus behind our cottage, or a unicorn came prancing through the waterfall, you wouldn't be surprised.

Elijah felt the magic. Followed by Alex, he climbed onto the parapet of the cottage roof, which had a narrow ledge wide enough to stand on, spread out his arms and crowed, 'I'm the king of the castle.'

Robert yelled: 'Alex, get down. It's not safe up there.'

We had sausages and chips for supper.

'Why'd you only call Alex down?'

'Don't be silly.' I ruffled Elijah's hair. Only you can't ruffle kinky hair. Your hand glides through and the hair stays the same. I'd never touched his curls before; they felt dry almost scaly.

Robert said: 'Come on, boys, let's unpack the car.'

Robert, grim-faced, humped in our suitcase. The caterpillar strings on the luggage rack had worked loose and two items had fallen off, one, a carton with extra pillows and, as luck would have it, the other, Elijah's suitcase. 'We gotta go back. We gotta.' He was waving his arms, squealing.

'But Elijah – it's blown away on the Motorway, we'd never find it. Tomorrow, we'll go out first thing and buy you some new stuff.'

'Nah, I gotta have them things. Me Mum bought 'em.' He rolled up his eyes. He looked yellow; he looked ill.

Robert said: 'Don't fuss, Elijah. Accidents happen. You'll get them replaced.'

He wouldn't look at us; he wouldn't speak to us.

'When we goin' back for my suitcase? When?' Elijah narrowed his eyes. Looked straight at me. Then the popping noise of a fart. And then lightning following thunder – the smell. Methane, rotten eggs. sulphur. No human being – let alone a child, could make such a stink?

Alex held his nose and said, 'Pooey!'

How can you tell a child off for a fart, in a tiny cottage with the windows shut. We ate in silence.

Elijah laid down his fork, picked up the salt cellar, reversed it over his sausages. He went on pouring until both went frosted. The very sight made you gag.

'Elijah?'

'What?'

'There's too much salt on your food.'

'Nah! I likes salt.'

Robert had opened the door and was fanning a newspaper to try and get out the smell. In between each bite, Elijah hummed: 'Da-da-di-di-di- da- to the sound of music...' He ate a slice of sausage and speared a chip. Open, close, chew, swallow, hum: 'Da-da-di-di-di- da- to the sound of music...' Eleven syllables. The performance carried on until his plate was empty. He must have hummed at least a dozen times. He was a slow eater.

Robert closed the door. Poured himself a whiskey. Usually he wouldn't take a drink until after the kids were in bed. 'I suppose that was an accident?' he said.

The cottage has only two rooms. Upstairs, there's a double bed and a bunk bed along the whitewashed wall. I always meant to string up a curtain to separate the bed and the bunk but it's not like Robert and I are in the first flush of sex, we'd already had our Silver Anniversary the year before Elijah came. so we can abstain when children are sleeping in earshot. We didn't mind peeing upstairs. We had two potties, one under the bunk, one under the bed and also a chemical lav in a shed behind the cottage. We pee outside often. We love it. Back to Nature. Although you can only go back to nature to some extent, we are still civilised. That's what Elijah didn't seem to realise.

Next morning he was all smiles – worries over the lost suitcase forgotten. We bought him a pair of jeans, a blue sweater, two tee shirts and a pair of gumboots.

'Suppose he lets one off?' I whispered.

Robert whispered back, 'He won't. Just trying us out.'

'And who's this fine boy, then?' Mrs Jones admired Elijah, a young leopard in his new outfit.

'He is a sort of, a sort of... foster son,' said Robert. Well, that did surprise me.

Back at the cottage, I unpacked Elijah's new clothes and gave Alex the Teddy we'd bought him.

Elijah said: 'A Teddy? That's sissy.'

Alex threw the Teddy under the bunk.

Robert said, 'Who wants a game of chess?'

Elijah sat down. I started supper. Alex coloured in his magic colouring book.

'Mate, I think,' announced Robert after a few moves. He does like to win, even playing with a child.

Elijah jumped up. The board tipped; several pieces fell onto the slate floor.

'Steady on,' cried Robert.

'S'boring,' said Elijah and farted. Was it something to do with the huge amounts of salt? Could he do it at will?

'If you want to do Number Two, you must go outside,' I said holding my jaw so tight my teeth ached.

'I don't need to,' said Elijah and hummed gently,: 'Da-da-di-di-di-da-to the sound of music...' and went on humming for fifteen minutes.

Next evening I was alone with the two boys, rolling out pastry. 'Now let's lay the table for supper. Alex, get the glasses, please.'

The glasses were on the second shelf of the Welsh dresser. Alex needed the stool. I didn't see what happened. The stool somehow fell; Alex dropped two glasses. Robert came back just as I was sweeping up the pieces. Alex was sniffling.

'You're an idiot, Alex. Why didn't you wait until I got home?'

'Should 'ave asked me. I'm taller,' said Elijah.

I'd been rather fond of those glasses – part of a wedding present set. Elijah couldn't have pushed that stool over, could he? He was standing on the other side of the room.

We had Steak and Kidney pud and chips. Elijah did the salt trick again. It snowed over the pastry. It snowed over the slices of tomato until the plate was frosted. The muscles in my buttocks tensed: I was not going to say a word.

Elijah used his knife and fork neatly, the salted food portioned into neat chunks and conveyed to his mouth without any drips.

'Look how nicely Elijah cuts up his food, Alex. Why don't you try?'

Alex sawed at pieces of pie crust so hard that it leapt the plate and crashed into Elijah's lap.

''Ere, leave off,' said Elijah.

I snapped, 'It was an accident. You know about those.'

Robert said: 'Sure you need so much salt, Elijah? It's bad for your kidneys, you know.'

Elijah turned his large black eyes towards first me, then Robert, looking like a wounded doe. The smell hit five seconds later. Robert stiffened. I kicked his ankle.

Alex said: 'I can't eat in this poo-ey room,' and ran upstairs.

Elijah cut, swallowed and chewed and after each swallow came the same eleven notes; 'Da-da-di-di-di- da-to the sound of music... Da-da-di-di-di- da-to the sound of music...'

You remember Room 101? The room in George Orwell's novel that the torturers put you when they have discovered whatever it is you can't stand. Elijah had discovered our Room 101. Sounds ridiculous, doesn't it? Sounds silly. A routine straight from Hell; fart, salt, hum. Every meal time, watch someone cover the food until it was white as death, smell that terrible stench and listen to the same eleven notes repeated over and over. Over and over until you wanted to scream.

We whispered under the bedclothes. 'What'll we do if he lets off up here? I'll suffocate.'

I stroked Robert's back. 'He won't. It's only a test. We'll have passed in a day or so.'

'We're bloody well failing,' muttered Robert.

'No, we aren't. It'll be fine. You'll see.'

And I wanted to believe it.

News spreads fast in a valley. Everyone knows everyone else's business or thinks that they do. It's still a face-to-face society. One of our neighbours was a widow, the daughter of a famous suffragette, whose hobby, the daughter's, not the suffragette's, was using up bin ends, so her bobble hats, gloves and scarves were always knitted in bands of violently clashing colours.

'So this is our new arrival. Hill-oo, my dear.' Elijah flashed a smile. Julia was duly charmed. No, she wouldn't stay for a cup of coffee but, 'Now that we have met, I'll get knitting straightaway.'

The battle of wills continued. Every meal time, Elijah salted his food white, let off at least two farts and hummed until we heard bees in our brains. He held us in the palm of his hand or was it the twitching of his sphincter? Whatever was said he didn't like or whatever he was asked to do that he didn't want to, he'd let off a fart. It didn't seem possible that the thirty-odd kilos he must have weighed, could manufacture so much gas.

'What next?' I asked Robert. We were in the second week of a four-week holiday.

'Search me,' replied Robert. 'We can't tell anyone; we'd sound such Charlies. It's so fiendish.'

'There has to be some solution. What does he do it for?'

'Ask him,' said Robert.

Next morning I was trying to think of some way to broach the subject, when Julia knocked. She'd brought an olive green, mauve and pink scarf for Elijah. 'A brisk blow up and over, that's what we need. Such a beautiful day.'

It was – one of those rare days at the end of February with mountains etched purple on the horizon, white exclamation marks of sheep on the hills, the smell of Spring and the sound of waterfalls.

'Look at that cute black sheep up there, Elijah,' Julia wound the scarf around his neck. 'That's where we are going. Up and up.'

Elijah gave her a doe-eyed look. 'My, won't he make the gals sit up!' Elijah held Julia's hand. She was a dumpy woman so that they almost of a height. They walked ahead at a brisker pace than mine, with their heads close together, Elijah whispering in her ear. Julia turned to look at me, suspicion etching creases down either side of her mouth.

I tried to stride faster, determined not to let this, this child rile me. The path grew too steep to walk abreast. We dropped into single file, Elijah and Julia far ahead – almost at the summit. We toiled towards them. Alex had dropped right behind.

Up at the top the wind blows hard. When you look down the village is Toytown and the sight terrifies me; heights scare me. I clung onto Robert. Alex was whining below. 'I'm stuck.' Julia gave us a pitying look and said, 'I'll fetch him.'

Like a monster pixie, she scrambled past me, dislodging pebbles. 'Com – ing, Alex. Don't you be a-scared. I'm on my wa-a-a-y.'

A cairn of pebbles marked the summit. Elijah clambered on top and capered.

Robert snapped, 'Come down, you fool. You'll fall.' Elijah capered some more. 'I said down.' Elijah thumped his chest. 'Stop acting like a monkey.'

Elijah jumped off the heap of stones, crouched on all fours and spat: 'You fuckin', religious nutter – makin' us say prayers. Yer think yer're God. I know what you are.' A string of the most terrible swear words followed. Where could a child have learnt such words!

'Stop that,' said Robert. He'd gone white.

Elijah looked over our heads, saw Julia and stopped.

'Here's our boy,' she cried, panting from the effort of carrying Alex piggy-back.

''Oh, really Julia, you shouldn't have done that,' said Robert. 'He could've managed by himself.' He turned to Elijah: 'Get along now, we're all going down. And you, too, you little perisher.' Understandable if you had heard the insults. Julia hadn't.

Elijah huddled himself into a ball. 'I'm scared, Julia 'cos he hits me.'

'Little liar!' I gasped.

Julia clasped Elijah against her anorak, his eyelashes curved like question marks along his high cheekbones, their very symmetry accusing us. The pair scurried ahead hand in hand. We had to half-drag, half-cajole Alex down the mountainside. The wind blew cold. Alex's cheeks were pale and he had smudges under his eyes.

Back at the cottage, Julia was waiting. No, she wouldn't stay for a cup of tea. She pressed Elijah's hands in both hers. 'Courage, my dear, courage. Goodbye, Sara, goodbye, Robert. I'll be back tomorrow. We have things to discuss.'

Rage lumped in my chest like a swollen cork, which I ached to pull out.

Elijah began crayoning in Alex's colouring book pressing so deep he tore holes in the paper. Robert said: 'That belongs to Alex.'

Elijah closed the book gently. We waited. The farts didn't come. Only 'Da-da-di-di-di- da-to the sound of music...' sixty-two times (I know – I counted) hummed in a tone so inaudible that I couldn't swear whether the noise came from Elijah or from inside my skull.

Next morning, without a word, Robert and I started to pack – ten days left but the holiday had gone sour. The children didn't ask why we were leaving. Alex left the new Teddy under the bunk.

Robert pinned a note for Julia to the front door. 'Let the old buzzard think what she chooses.'

On the journey home, Elijah behaved so sweetly that I began to doubt my memories. He played I-Spy with Alex. At 'The Happy Eater,' he left the salt packets alone and ate his hamburger like everyone else. He said: 'Me Mum'll beat me fer those clothes.'

'Of course she won't. And you have those lovely new ones to show her.'

'Nah,' said Elijah. He held out his wrists. Two pencil-thin scars braceleted the golden skin. 'Me Mum did that,' he said, 'with piano wire.'

'Elijah?' His head turned away, pressing his forehead against the car window.

We were home before dark. Robert and I carried in the luggage and left the boys outside.

A single scream – Alex's voice. We ran.

The ginger cat lay on the gravel, its back legs twitching, its head at an impossible angle. The stone had smashed into one eye. Rage erupted. I reached out for Elijah and shook his thin shoulders until his head rattled. 'You little bastard. You murdering, little, black bastard.' Where had the words come from?

He didn't cry; he didn't flinch. 'I didn't do nothink. He did!'

Robert had Alex pressed against his chest, Elijah's catapult hanging from his hand.

Alice refused to take Elijah. 'I did warn you,' she said. 'Try his mother. Here's her number.'

The princess spoke English with almost no accent. Yes, she could take the 9 a.m. train from London. Yes, she would be with us before eleven-thirty. 'And thank you so much, so much, for taking care of my son.'

Elijah appeared asleep when I looked in. I don't know whether he'd heard my telephone voice from our bedroom. Robert always says I raise my voice when speaking to foreigners.

I fried Elijah's favourite sausages for breakfast – his last in our house. When I went to wake him, he wasn't in bed. How could he get out? Where could he go? It didn't need a Sherlock Holmes. The flower bed had a muddy footprint. He'd jumped out from the first floor. My God, he could've killed himself! A child can't be that scared!

The Police sergeant held a German Shepherd bitch on a leash. Alex wanted to pet her. 'Of course you can, Sonny,' the sergeant said. 'Just let's have a decko round here first.'

'But I've told you – he's not here. His mother is due. Now.'

'Now don't you fret, Madam. Missing kids generally turn up near the home.'

'This isn't his home.'

Robert backed out the car to fetch the princess from the station.

The dog had quartered every square inch of our house and garden. Finding no evidence that we'd bumped him off or hidden him somewhere, the police grew friendlier. 'These checks – standard precaution, Madam.'

The police dog had tracked Elijah into the allotments then lost the scent. My thoughts were whirling, kidnap, rape, murder, when Robert ushered in the princess – a golden edition of Elijah. She couldn't have been older than twenty-five; she could have passed for eighteen. She appeared poised, unruffled and unemotional. She showed no surprise, worry or alarm. 'He has done such things before, you know. He is a child with much evil inside him.' Her fingernails were long and lacquered gold. Could there be any truth in Elijah's lies? This was ridiculous. Those exquisite hands could never torture.

The Police left; they would keep us informed.

Robert and I sat facing the princess and fidgeted. The Princess Amina sat with upright back, her feet crossed at the ankle, her hands folded into her lap. She made one remark, 'He saw them kill his father,' she said.

'Where's Alex?' asked Robert.

I found him uprooting stones from the rockery and dragging them to line a hole he had dug under a tree. He was burying the rat. I tried to make him come inside. I tried to kiss him. He wouldn't let me.

The phone rang at 12.09. Four hours and nine minutes. The call was from Sergeant MacIndoe. They had found Elijah. He had telephoned the Samaritans from the callbox opposite the allotments.

'I've shut him in the cells for a coupla hours,' said the kindly policeman. 'Give 'im a bit of a fright like.' Then he added, 'Bit of a problem, the boy refuses point blank ter see 'is Mum. Starts carrying on as soon as we suggests it.'

They were not going to force him. They had telephoned the school, the Housemaster was driving over to pick him up. For the police the matter was closed. No one blamed us. No one held us responsible. No one was going to do anything. I kept telling myself – no one held us responsible.

The princess listened – face impassive as a golden mask while I told her. She asked could she smoke. I nodded. She didn't want to be driven to the station, she preferred a taxi. She took away the cheap suitcase and the items that I'd bought to replace Elijah's lost clothes and didn't offer to pay. Robert wouldn't have accepted anyway.

The Housemaster rang six months later. Elijah wanted to speak to us. The social worker had warned us this might happen. We had decided beforehand on our response – not to speak to him. What could we have said? We didn't want him back – not in our home. Not after the cat incident. Can a child be evil? Surely not. I don't want to think about the cat. Horror has no place in my garden. I've never even seen a length of piano wire.

We've never heard from Elijah again. He must be a handsome young man by now. My Gran used to say: 'It's not our great crimes that haunt us – it's our petty ones.'

In Our Tribe
the Women
are not Shepherds

In our tribe women are not shepherds. Because of the mark, I have become one. Because of the mark, I am shunned. No one dares to look upon my full face. My disfigurement reaches from my hairline and spreads to its widest point across my left cheek before it tapers and disappears into the hollow of my collarbone. The mark shows only on the left side of my face; seen from the right, nothing distinguishes me from any other village woman – short, dark and sallow-skinned.

We are as unlike in our bodies, as in our timid behaviour, from the blue-eyed Northerners, who have (beyond living memory) swept across the plains on their annual raids. They steal our harvest, sometimes take a woman, sometimes a child. I have never feared them; the curse of my mark protects me.

That night, we heard their ponies whinny, the unshod hooves thudding through our narrow street. We pulled our blankets over our heads, waiting to hear a woman's shriek, stifled by a hand thrust across her mouth or the crackle of flames catching the roof beams. That night, we heard nothing. In the grey dawn light we crept out from our houses. My neighbour's dog sprawled in the ditch, its neck broken from one lash of their long-handled whips. We asked one another why they had come so early in the year, and where, on what dreadful errand, they had gone?

During its brief Spring, our sun-bitten land wears a fragile beauty, as hills turn a tender, piercing green and gold, the sky a luminous blue. As I drove the sheep upwards, the leading ewe's bell mingled with the high, sweet sound of an unseen skylark. I clambered over rocks that had rolled down from the mountain during winter avalanches, seeing clear signs that last night, the horsemen had ridden this way, for small stones dislodged by galloping hooves lay against the rockface. Nuggets of horse dung were still fresh. The sheep and my two dogs were out of sight around the next bend, where the land rises into a smooth mound that we call the Virgin's Breast. The younger of the dogs, a piebald bitch, yelped. I whistled lest she scatter the sheep. She disobeyed. Her barks bounced off rocks and echoed down the valley. I snatched up a stick and ran to beat her into silence. I found her standing splay-legged, her hackles raised, barking at something which lay in the shadow of a rock. At first I thought it must be a dead sheep killed by a wolf.

On the summit of the Virgin's Breast, a man lay face down, his arms outstretched, half-naked like a statue of the Christians' god. Like him, he had suffered a terrible mutilation. From the nape of his neck to the cleft in his buttocks, the skin was slashed open in one long sweep. They must have used a knife of finest steel for the cut went straight with no jagged edge. Two flaps of skin were ripped apart as far as his armpits into triangular-shaped wings, held fast to the ground with two yellow rocks. Too early in the year for flies, six buzzards circled overhead, waiting.

I crouched down; the man, his head turned to one side, was still alive. I hurled the blood-splashed yellow rocks into the ravine. Trying to still the trembling of my hands, I laid the curled flaps of skin over the gaping wound. I bound them in place with my white scarf. The man moaned, his head rocked from side to side. Curious and strange to see behind his matted hair, that most delicate of Spring blooms – a cyclamen, flutter its pink petals.

I hoisted him upon my back. From his leather boots and breeches I judged that he must be one of them. To retrace the path took me six hours with the wounded man bumping against me, heavy as a half-dead sheep, his lashed wrists almost choking me. The heavy gold armbands that he wore, bruised my shoulders. Why had his torturers not removed them? I worried for my beasts, left unattended on the mountain pasture. The dogs slunk at my heels. As always happens when I make a gross effort, the mark throbbed. I knew it had turned an ugly purple.

I carried the man to my hut, laid him down and went in search of my brothers. Three of the five came. One held his legs. The other two positioned themselves right and left of the bed and tied the man's arms to two stakes which they held upright. Weakened as he was, his struggles were no more than a worm squirming upon a pin – until he felt my needle pierce through the flaps of skin. With his mouth gagged, the strength of his screams could only be felt as I stitched them together, tautening and knotting each stitch, as I had once seen an Arab physician do. My sisters-in-law leaned in the doorway. 'Wrench off those armbands,' they cried. Their covetous eyes fixed upon the six, worked in gold as heavy as a chief wears, wound tight around his upper arms. I shook my head. They pulled aside their veils, spat and said he would shortly die. He groaned, as I dripped warm water onto the clots of blood to soften and wipe them away. I heaped up a bed of dried ferns. Less soft than a cotton-filled mattress but easy to renew when fouled or bloodied. With such injuries, he must soon die.

We have learnt little magnanimity from our poverty. With envy, we watch, from our flat roof tops, year by year, in early summer, the heavy-laden mules and camels of the silk caravans cross the valley floor far below us. Rich as they are, they pay tribute to the Northmen and are left alone. We, who have nothing, can neither barter with the merchants, nor escape the horsemen's raids. Our countryside is barren, our weaving crude, our goats skinny. Yet we possess one plant of great worth and rarity. A spiny bush half as high as a man, grows in the most inaccessible places hidden on the mountainside, where only we can find it. In September, its purple berries swell and ripen; their juice contains amazing curative properties. We are rarely able to collect more than a cupful. But this year, the shaman (who is as poor as the rest of us) had long desired one of the red-bordered silk robes the caravan carries on its long journey from China. Towards this goal, he had sent teams of boys into the hills to find the bush. The berries yielded enough juice to fill a leather bottle. Such an amount appeared magical in our eyes. All winter we had marvelled, whenever the shaman held up his prize. Duty warred with desire, as he offered : 'Maritsa, use my flask to tend the horseman's wounds.' Like me he assumed the stranger was one. Was it the blue of those vacant eyes or the bowed calves that must have gripped a horse's flanks since early childhood? Because the shaman had made a holy sacrifice, I bowed and received the bottle in my two cupped hands.

Every morning and evening, I sprinkled exactly seven drops of the precious juice onto a wadded cloth and squeezed them onto the taut black threads of the stitched wounds. I placed him upon his left side to tend him. His eyes followed my movements but he would never speak. Eyes so empty – as if they had seen something so terrible – they did not wish to see again. But under my care the swollen flesh shrank. When the edges of puckered skin had joined, I pulled the threads out one by one and burned them; they seemed unlucky. My foresight to provide a bed of dried ferns was good, frequently in those first weeks, the wounded man passed pellets, hard and shiny like a sheep's. Day by day, the damage to his body healed: the damage to his mind remained. What crime could he have committed so terrible to have undergone such a punishment? Whom had he dishonoured? He must have dishonoured someone; honour is their god. When he would be well enough to speak, he must tell me.

High summer had come and gone; apricots were drying on the roofs. Behind the mountains the first blizzards were waiting. The shaman, in spite of the loss of his silk robe, took a lively interest in the man whom he said we must call Guruk, which in our language means Unlucky One. Daily, the shaman visited my hut. I wished to stop him but I could not. He of all people – should not see my face. Although I tried to keep my head turned aside, he could not avoid seeing the mark. It was shrinking. The striated skin smoothed and lost its wicked purple; the raised edges folded in upon themselves. When I smiled the side of my mouth no longer skewed sideways. When he saw this, the shaman sucked his teeth as though he were hissing. Then he bowed as low as if he were officiating at the altar. Many times during the last thirty-five years he had performed incantations over my head, smeared chickens' blood over my cheeks. His cures effected nothing. His efforts had cost my parents many hides. After their death, they ceased. My sisters were married elsewhere; my brothers held out smiling hands and kept their eyes turned away. Now, as the shaman strutted around the village to spread the astonishing news, I was praised and petted and invited to sit in the place of honour to drink innumerable cups of mint tea. Pregnant women no longer turned their backs. Would my luck rub off onto them? 'See how softened she has become,' they cried to one another.

The shaman took full credit for the miracle. 'She has healed the sick through my instruction and the Gods have pardoned her.'

Guruk had taken to following at my heels as close as the piebald bitch. His arms had lost their full range of movement. Although his sturdy body returned to health, he either would not, or dared not, speak.

My eldest brother brought me a red and black woollen robe embroidered with so many beads and mirrors that it could stand like an empty statue by itself. This robe he spread out across my bed and departed without looking at my altered face, although I knew that he had seen. Neither wishing, nor needing this robe, I feared the reason for the gift.

Preparations began for the harvest festival and for some other ceremony that had been decided by the village council. My consent was not asked, nor was I spoken to by any of the Elders. Outside my hut, they erected an arch garlanded with leaves and harvest fruits.

Guruk tried to run away. I believe he thought that we intended to sacrifice him, along with the goats he saw slaughtered in the street. The men caught him before he had gone farther than the stone cairn that marks the outer limits of the village. Laughing, they brought him back tied to a mule's tail.

His flight had induced a slight fever in Guruk. 'Tend him. Tend him well,' cried the men. I washed his hair with calomel leaves. It amused me to see the fine light tendrils float upon his shoulders. His fever soon abated. My mark shrank further and further, until it became little more than a discoloration, no more than a blush upon my cheek.

'Maritsa is handsome,' cried the shaman. 'A miracle, a miracle.' Smiling vanity settled on his broad foolish face. In return my face smiled also. There was no miracle. No Gods had blessed me. Why should they? Whenever I finished swabbing Guruk's wound with the juice, I had rubbed my fingers around the edges of the mark, spreading the moisture over the coils of discoloured flesh, kneading and pressing until my hands ached. The juice stung. Its smell I can never forget. Its essence filled my head in a way the shaman's songs had never done.

'So, Maritsa,' said my brother's wife. 'Now you will be married and learn to obey.'

The week before the wedding the shaman carried Guruk off to his own house, saying it was not fitting he should continue to sleep beneath the ridge pole of his future wife. His gibbers and moans disturbed the peace of the shaman's wives. With Guruk gone, the image of his face, his high-bridged nose and his blue, blue eyes would not leave me. I seemed to see him everywhere. And it was then, that I recalled what I'd seen without noticing, the shame in Guruk's eyes when his gaze crossed mine. Was he, from his armbands, evidently, a great warrior, ashamed to be tended by a woman, a disfigured one at that? No, that was not his shame. His shame lay elsewhere. If he would not speak, I knew who would. Only one man goes from our puny village to the plains where the Northmen pitch their tents. I called the salt-peddler and gave him much wine.

With my bitch curled at the end of my bed, I slept well, my mind made-up. The night before the wedding, I waited until every householder slept. As I stepped from pool to pool of shadow, my hood, once again, as in the days of my mark, shielded my face.

The shaman's swiftest pony was a flea-bitten grey mare. I stuffed her saddlebags with barley cakes and slung two water skins from the back of the saddle. In the shaman's house, Guruk slept huddled against the warmth of the firestones.

In the morning when they came for me, Guruk was gone!

The women, married to men like my brothers or worse, scream and shout, so angry that I shall escape their state. 'You are doubly cursed. Your mark will return.'

I do not think so; my smile sits easy. When my mark disfigured me, I had no choice. Now I am free and will remain so. Not so for Guruk. The salt peddler has told me that, some months ago, a girl was stoned to death by the Northerners. That is their penalty for a woman's dishonour. For the man concerned, the penalty is yet more terrible. The dead girl was the chief's daughter. Their chiefs wear six gold armbands. Oh, Guruk, do I remind you of a dishonoured woman?

With his crippled arms, Guruk cannot ride for more than two days. Let him die in the mountains. I know why the horsemen spread-eagled him. Now that I am free, I shall remain so.

-oOo-

Duet
for
Three Voices

Sonya: 12.55p.m. It started as a joke.

Si says to me while we were washing up the breakfast dishes that he's never seen one. So I say: come up to my room before lunch and I'll show you mine. So I did. His eyes went glassy like boiled sweets. He touched the tip with his thumb and jerked back like he's been stung. Bloody idiot! The blush looked ugly on that apricot skin of his. But it made me want to kiss the hollow between his neck and collarbone. He arched himself on all fours, high above me. Suddenly, he seemed too big and I shoved him as hard as I could in the chest and yelled, 'Get out.'

Why the hell doesn't Sybil have keys to her doors? I need a locked door. With the curtains drawn the room's green – an underwater cave. I creep underneath the duvet; the Indian coverlet goes over my head. Blessed long fingers. One finger and a thumb. Who says there's no G-spot?

Oh, no! I can't! I can't!. I can't! I can't forget those bastards.

Simon: 1p.m. I'd no idea. It was standing up by itself – red like a miniature prick with a cute little hood over the top. Such a big lady keeping that cute little thing tucked between her thighs. She had wavy hairs on her thighs. She let me touch the tip. I felt like it scalded my thumb. I tried to kiss her, Her lips puckered. Was she cross? Did I do something wrong? God, I'd like to have...

Sybil: 1.07p.m. Where the hell are they? Lunch is planned for 1p.m. sharp. Everyone knows I run this house like clockwork. Not a sound coming from upstairs. Lunch will get cold. Tsk, tsk, it won't. It's cold already. Hard-boiled eggs and beetroot salad. Why does beetroot look so shameless?

Poor little Sonya. Not so little. Must be a good ten inches taller than me. Weighs over eleven stone I don't doubt. She'll be fat when she's my age. I'm sure she's getting better here. She must be. For a start she isn't smoking like a chimney . That's a good sign. If only I could force her to talk about it. Get it out of her system. Talking makes things better. I should know. She won't. Clams up whenever I poke, oh, so gently.

The delphs look ever so pretty the way I've arranged them on the mantelpiece. And the table looks a treat. Not that they'll say. One mustn't expect gratitude from the young – that's what I've learnt. Take, take, take, that's all they know. Think the world belongs to them.

Where is Simon? Can't be healthy for a boy his age, moping round the house all day alone with two women. He should go out more. I never encouraged him when he was younger. I didn't like him going out; it's safer at home.

Of course if Harold hadn't... I could've seen it coming – a man like that. I did the right thing. I've got nothing to reproach myself for.

Well, past is past. Water under the bridge as Gran would've said. She'd say – no use crying over spilt milk. As good fish in the sea as ever came out. There's a deal of sense in those old sayings. That's why they last.

Where are they?

Simon: 1.07p.m. What am I going to do with these dam pants? Mum'll see the wet bit. If I rinse 'em out, she'll ask why. Does she have to be so nosy?

- You're all that's left to me, Si.

Crap. 'S'not my fault Dad buggered off.

Sonya: 1.10p.m. Straighten bedclothes. Brush hair. Lipstick. Ok, I look fine. Si's so sweet. Don't fool yourself, gel. You're twenty-nine. Stranger things have happened. Not in dear Aunt Sybil's house! Even the books wouldn't dare lean out of line. And Mum says she was so sweet as a girl...

Sybil: 1.15p.m. They haven't any respect. This isn't a hotel. How long is she going to stay? I didn't offer an indefinite stay. Or did I? I said: – After your terrifying ordeal, Sonya, you must come and recuperate – with us. We're family. This is a quiet neighbourhood. No one to bother you. No men. Si doesn't count.

Simon: 1.20p.m. God, I'm hungry and I hate beetroot. Why's Mum staring?

Sybil: 1.20p.m. What am I supposed to talk about? There's been some funny business going on, I bet you.

Simon: 1.21 p.m. So I ask Mum how's Maria and she says, toffee-nosed, 'You know that your sister never complains.'
   - Not typical of our family then, is she?
   - What do you mean? Mum's eyes stretch wide; they almost pop out of her head. She's probably waggling her ears but her hair covers them.

Sonya: 1.22p.m. I ask whether Maria is coming back during the holidays. Why the hell do I? I know that she's not. She can't face her mother, which is utterly unreasonable. What happened isn't Sybil's fault. Whose fault is it? But I shouldn't stay here without Maria. Sybil's brought coffee out on the terrace. She can't let up; lace mats and sugar tongs even for us.

Simon: 1.30p.m. I want to get Sonya alone again. How'm I gunna do it? Look at her stretched out in that deckchair with her tits flopping on either side. She doesn't shave her legs or her armpits. I could smell when she stretched across for the bread – sweetish like rancid oil. God, if only I could. Just once. 'Spose I died and I hadn't even done it. Done it just once to know what it's like...

Sybil: 1.30p.m. How can I break this silence; it weighs on me like a leather bag filled with stones.

Sonya: 1.40p.m. The sun strokes my eyelids. Healing. Aunt Sybil's listening to The Archers. Appropriate. Sharon's left John 'cos she's older. When you're in some sort of situation everything reminds you. Funny.

Simon: 1.42p.m. If I move my leg I could just touch hers.

Sybil: 1.43p.m. I can't stand watching them not look at each other any longer.

- Si, run upstairs. I need my library book. Don't make that face. Just go.

Definitely a mistake that indefinite stay. I've never been one who refuses to acknowledge my mistakes. Harold included. I'll just find a good excuse. I don't want to hurt her feelings. She's been hurt enough. Still, that's not the sort of influence I want for my boy. Look at that blouse! Plenty to show and she's showing every bit of it.

Simply I'll say, 'You know the spare room needs redecorating before term starts.' She'll understand. It's not as though she has nowhere else to go.

Simon: 1.50p.m. The old cow! I'll kill her. She can't ask Sonya to go. I won't let her. Fuck the spare room. It doesn't need painting. She said that Sonya's been ill; that she needs a rest. She's only been here for two weeks. There's lots and lots of things I want to show her. I said I'd take her to the New Leisure Centre. There's lots and lots of things that she could show me.

Sonya: 1.50p.m. She can't be serious! She can't mean that she wants me to go back to that flat on my own. Not yet I can't. Not where they did it. On the white rug. The judge said that I shouldn't have asked them in for coffee. But they worked in Maria's office. The fat one said he was married.

I can't stay if she wants the spare room. That green is pretty horrible. Why doesn't Simon say something? He's supposed to be so fond of me.

Suspicions? She can't have any. Nothing has happened. How could it? That'd be stupid. We haven't done anything. I told her when I came that I'll never want a man to touch me again. Ever. She laughed like she didn't believe me but she looked pleased. I bet she's never liked it. Maybe that's why Uncle Harold...

The dandelions on the lawn are grinning. What at?

I can go back; I can take an extra Valium. I can chain the front door...

Simon: 1.51p.m. Brainwave! I'm a genius. It can't possibly happen. It'd be too marvellous. Things like that only happen in films. But I can. But I can ask her. She can only say – no. Or she could, she could only say – yes. Yes, Simon, I should love us to travel to Brixton together.

Mum wants to listen to the Afternoon Play; I can get away easy. I'll carry her suitcases. Damn, she hasn't got any. Only those plastic bags. I'll carry those. We could go out and see a film once she's unpacked the plastic bags. Then it'd be too late to catch the last tube home. She'd have to invite me to stay over.

Sybil: 1.52p.m. This is crazy; the situation is running out of control. It's her I wanted to get shut of. He can't go with her. Not to Brixton. That's a dangerous area. Full of foreigners. She had no business buying a flat there. Nor sharing with Maria. He can't go. I shall put my foot down. Anyway, he's promised to mow the lawn. It's covered in dandelions. Then he promised to return my library books. They're overdue. I hate paying fines. He wants to carry her luggage on the Underground.

Haven't they heard of taxis?

It's me that told her to leave. Made it awkward for her to stay. What shall I do now? I can't stop him going. He's only a child. Only a child. Nothing can possibly happen. Of course it can't. She wouldn't allow it. Not after what she's been through. She's not a pervert.

He's getting so tall. He's getting so...

Sonya: 1.52p.m. He doesn't look me in the eyes. I shouldn't have let him. It was wrong. And now he said, can I come with you? I said, sure. I shouldn't have said sure. But he is so sweet. Isn't he sweet? Those blackheads bulging on the side of his nose. I could squeeze them if he'd let me. Two fingers. Apply pressure. Skin stretches. Black head pops out followed by the waxy greasy tail wiggling like a worm. More pressure. The worm doubles back on itself and dies. An empty, reddened hole. Everything clean again.

Afterwards I thought that I'd never get clean. So much Dettol I burnt myself. The police surgeon couldn't get proper evidence because of the burns. I didn't care. I was glad. I wanted the burns deep inside.

The judge blamed me for asking them in. Bloody Hell! Maria knew them!

Aunt Sybil looked daggers when Si suggested taking my luggage. I haven't got any. Just those carriers. She shouldn't be so possessive.

I mean, suppose something did happen? Of course it won't. I mean, he's only a kid. He's practically my kid brother. Maria's my mate. Suppose something did. The hollow between his neck and collarbone, I want to sink my teeth in. Sonya the vampire. Why not?

I couldn't hurt Si. I couldn't. Gently, gently, little coz. Not like they hurt me. I couldn't ever do it with a man again. Si's a boy, isn't he? I'll get over them. He'll help me. I'll help him. We don't have to say anything. Nothing need be said. It'll happen just by itself – if it's meant to.

Simon: 1.53p.m. Sonya says, yes. Sonya says that I can take her back to her flat. What'll I say? What'll I say to her in the tube? How can I make something happen? I'm gunna buy flowers. A whole big bunch of daffs. Is it the season for daffs? Roses'd be better. I can take her to the door of the flat and say, hang on a sec, I need a packet of fags. That won't work. She knows that I don't smoke. I can say, wait a sec, I'll fetch us the evening paper. Then back I trot with the flowers – arms full of flowers and I say...

Anything can happen.

Maybe it will.

Sybil: 3.0p.m. They've gone! The house is silent except for the kitchen tap dripping. Need a man to fix it. The washer is worn through. With them leaving like that I missed the Afternoon Play – Drunk in the Afternoon. Suitable title. Bet I missed a good play.

She said – best to get it over with straightaway. And packed up and left. Get what over with? It didn't take her 45 minutes.

A snake have I harboured in my bosom.

I had such plans for my little niece. She could've bettered herself. Taken some further qualifications and stayed here while she studied. She could be something better than an SRN.

He's only sixteen.

Let's have another. Sherry is such a pretty colour, don't you think. That's better.

It's as silent as the grave in here.

The grave's a fine and silent place but none I think do there embrace. Harold used to quote that poem. Shakespeare or someone.

Hang on a sec – Sybil, my girl – how old were you?

How old was I? Scrumble-fumble on Mum's carpet and Harold not managing the thingy.

I was sixteen.

But this is different. Girls mature earlier than boys. My little boy. My own little boy. I rocked him like this in my arms.

I don't want another woman to...

He's not a little boy any longer. Not any more.

Chacun a son tour. My French was always excellent. What a pity there's no one left to appreciate it.

At least there's two tots left in the sherry bottle.

Cheers.

-oOo-

Playing the Game

A group of bare-breasted girls in brightly-coloured cotton lappas, slapping cloths against flat stones in the shallows, straightened their backs and waved as the heavy, black, government Humber swept beyond the bridge leading out of the capital.

'Oh, how charming, dear,' Muriel cried. Real Africa at last and in comfort, too.

Separated from the girls by a clump of feathery bushes, a group of men washing themselves in knee-deep water, turned their backs and waved gracefully over their shoulders.

'Charming,' repeated Muriel, winding down the window and waving back.

Her husband, Ronald, stared straight ahead. Samuel Odekunjo, his private secretary, bothered that she should see so much uncovered flesh, lit a cigarette. Ronald gave an ahemming cough. As Samuel lowered the window, a small boy darted from nowhere to grab the stub. Ronald cleared his throat.

'Enjoy yesterday's match, did you, old man?'

'Oh, absolutely, Sir,' Samuel's white teeth flashed an affirmative.

'Understand the rules, OK?'

'Oh, absolutely, Sir, Mrs Marchant was giving splendid explanation.'

Muriel thought: if he's not lying – I'm a monkey's uncle. They'd been squashed up against one another on a narrow bench, surrounded by rows of straw-hatted expat wives who were oozing like marzipan pigs in the heat of the grandstand.

Samuel wondered (in spite of his Mission education) whether he had appreciated or even understood what sport was about. Balls – the white races' obsession with the chasing of – on foot, in the water, on horseback, using bats, sticks and racquets and clubs. He found it somewhat odd, eight grown men galloping after a wooden ball in ninety-degree humidity while the sweat poured off them. He had obediently taken off his sunglasses when Mrs Marchant had grabbed his arm: 'Look, Ronnie's got the ball.' He had tried to show as much interest as possible, but, as he later explained to her in the tea break, he'd been calculating the value of the polo ground if, after Independence, it could be developed as a luxury office block. Mrs Marchant had looked quite cross when he had remarked that the site would be ever so valuable.

Muriel had not enjoyed her afternoon. 'His heart just wasn't in it,' she'd complained to Ronald, that evening, as they were changing for dinner. (A custom upon which Ronald insisted – even when they dined alone.)

'That's what we're here for. Show 'em how to play the game, old girl.'

Ronald had a stock of appropriate clichés for every situation but Africa she suspected, overwhelmed them. He'd shown great reluctance, taking her on this trip outstation but she'd insisted. 'I can't stay in the capital all the time.' So, here they were. Ronald in the middle, Samuel and herself on either side and the plastic cover over the leather seats crackling unpleasantly whenever they moved.

The Humber nosed its way further into the bush; the air-conditioning hummed. Before she had time to grow restless, the macadamised highway shrank to a single dirt track and trees in every conceivable shade of green engulfed the horizon. A canopy two hundred feet high arched above their heads.

The driver, avoiding potholes with unsettling wrenches of the wheel, steered straight into the path of an oncoming black snake zigzagging across the road. A slight bump. The snake's body curled like a squashed inner tube. When the men left the car, Ronald and Samuel on the right, the driver respectfully over on the other side, Muriel saw him buttoning up his trousers, stuffing inside the regulation khaki, a round-tipped something, flexible, broad and black as the dead snake's head. Ferns fanned out from the angles of branches; orchids clung to tree trunks, their purple horns summoning clouds of matching butterflies. She insisted that they stop; she had to stretch her legs.

'We've two hundred miles. Can't we get on?' snapped Ronald.

Once out of the car, the forest was surprisingly noisy: insects buzzed, whined, clicked and hummed; birds called urgently; monkeys screamed; disconcerting, hearing but not seeing them. Purple orchids came away into her eager hands in great sticky clumps. Shafting through layers of green, sunlight striped the broad leaves. She poked a stick into a crumbling earthen structure nearly as tall as she was – a termite nest. 'Aren't they clever little beasties, Ronnie?'

'Not very! For God's sake – you'll get stung!'

'Ouch!'

'See,' said Ronald, using his talent for stating the obvious.

'Oh, don't fuss.' Pretending the bite didn't hurt, she sauntered on down a track which led her into a clearing, where maize and cassava plants leant towards each other, nodding fringed heads like women gossiping at a well: a row of red and yellow-striped clay pots leant against the wall of a mudbrick hut, its palm thatch bare and skimpy. The clearing was not empty; from behind a palm tree, a woman with a baby on her back, was watching.

'He-llo, you funny little chap.' Muriel twiddled her fingers at the baby whose shaven skull glistened like polished ebony. 'Isn't he bonny, Ronnie?'

Ronald's swagger stick decapitated a cassava plant. 'Probably die soon as he's weaned.' Ronnie's red-rimmed, blue eyes glared at the remaining plants. 'Slash-burn, slash-burn, that's all they know. When will they learn! When! Heavens knows, I've tried.'

Indeed Muriel knew how hard he'd tried. That swagger stick and matching swagger hid a genuine kindness that she and she alone knew existed. He lacked confidence – that was his trouble; that was why he had to shout and bluster.

Samuel appeared ill-at-ease away from the car. The smart grey terylene suit he'd worn at yesterday's Polo match, looked silly in the forest. Not that they were much more comfortable, she in print frock already crumpled and Ronald, in khaki baggy shorts and woollen socks concertinaed over his ankles.

Filling her arms, the orchids appeared faded and flimsy; she threw them away. But she needed something from the forest; something to remind her she'd been there.

'Aren't those pots divine?'

'No trouble,' cried Samuel, 'no trouble at all,' and dashing forward, he scrabbled along the line – pots rolling in every direction. Choosing a wide, flat bowl with a pattern of orange lozenges, he bounced it like a baby into Muriel's arms. The woman remained behind her tree with downcast eyes; Samuel dropped a packet of cigarettes into her cupped hands.

'Bush people!' he said.

*

Ezeh, the District Officer, wearing an orange-flowered lappa knotted low onto his hips, waited in the pillared doorway of his house, holding a spray of jasmine diagonally across his bare chest; he was smoking a stubby cheroot. With an expansive gesture, Ezeh handed Muriel the branch of jasmine. At this, seven or eight barefoot children began clapping and singing, jigging up and down. A girl knocked Muriel's arm and a star-fall of white petals showered her skirt. 'No matter, no matter. Welcome, welcome for the V.I.Ps from our Capital. Welcome. My ever-so-humble home is yours.'

Muriel was taken aback. Humble? A mansion grand enough for a Permanent Secretary – but so shabby! Verandas sagging, walls crumbling, pillars shored up with metal posts. Monstrous banana leaves flapped against windows like giant hands threatening to come in.

Ezeh's teeth flashed. 'Please enter, I beg you.' Sweeping his arms in wide semi-circles, as though driving chickens into a coop, he ushered them onto a veranda. He shook a playful fist at the children, who backed outside and then hauled themselves up to the windowsills, their heads bobbing up and down like fairground coconuts. As dusk curved over the lagoon, lights started winking from both banks.

'I must be getting along,' said Samuel.

'Oh,' said Muriel, feeling nervous of Samuel's departure; he made a sort of bridge between Ronald and Ezeh, whom she found most peculiar. And she was going to need the toilet in a minute.

'I've booked room at Government Rest House, Sir,' said Samuel.

'Good show,' said Ronald. 'Expect you back here for chow. What time do we eat, Ezeh?'

Samuel's eyes slid from red-face to black-face and back again.

'Eight will do,' said Ezeh, seeming undisturbed by one guest inviting another for dinner. Samuel left; Muriel badly wanted a pee.

A youth wearing a white cotton jacket with its brass buttons done up lopsidedly, served warm beer on a tin tray. The boy's hands shook;

the liquid had slopped over the rims of the glasses.

'Dat boy never see white Madam in dis house before,' Ezeh grinned again. Muriel found him extraordinarily black.

Ronald, his cheeks puffed out in a great show of heartiness, began cracking jokes using, 'what,' every second sentence. Poor old Ronnie – not the pleasantest of situations, a guest whose probable actions would result in his host losing his job. Apparently no one in the ministry doubted this Ezeh person's guilt – only proof was needed. Muriel patted her husband's arm. Ronald would come up trumps. He had to! And let's hope he'd get the promotion he deserved. Independence only two years off and then what? What sort of post waited back Home for an ex-colonial officer of forty plus? This investigation must succeed. With another sip of luke warm beer, her bladder was starting to sting, investigation of toilet arrangements could no longer be delayed. She made appropriate noises. The yellow boy with a paraffin lamp in each hand, led them upstairs and her fears proved groundless; Ezeh had vacated the Master suite.

'Not bad, eh.' Ronald pressed a palm onto the sprung mattress. In the dressing room he pulled open cupboard doors and drawers still full of Ezeh's clothes. The bathroom astounded them both – an enormous enamel bath on clawed feet and, raised on a mahogany dais, a porcelain-bowled, mahogany-lidded lavatory which faced a brass-tapped washbowl surrounded with marble shelves.

'Fit for Queen Victoria.' Muriel's bladder emptied with relief. Bending over to wash her hands, she saw, reflected in the washbowl mirror, the blind eyes of a bronze mask, its thick lips curved upwards.

Ezeh, as they were themselves, was a public servant. Standard items from the Public Works Department furnished his rooms as did theirs. But out here, the conventional wooden tables, folding chairs and chests of drawers had changed. Each object was surrounded, almost hemmed-in by thick-lipped, worm-eaten statues. Muriel counted sixty before she gave up – the largest as big as a large monkey – the smallest the size of a doll but not any doll she had ever owned. They smelt of dust-laden age.

'They're frightfully creepy,' she said, sneezing.

'Museum pieces, some of 'em.' Ronald tested the weight of an ebony statue by banging it on the floor. 'Where's the money come from, 'eh? Not that rum goin's-on up here surprise me. Only stopped eatin' one another recently, what!'

'I wish you'd stop saying 'what', Ronnie.'

The flushing cistern drowned his next remark. Beneath tiers of noise, frogs' croaking, cicadas' clicking, laughter coming from the compound, a rhythmic boom-boom-boom penetrated the room. 'Isn't that noise a bit... ?'

What?'

'Oh, nothing.' She wouldn't admit the sound frightened her. 'Think I'll take a shower.'

A trickle of rust-coloured water dampened her hair. Two drips splashed her upturned eyes. The water stopped.

'Typical!' Ronald kicked the pipe and a decent flow emerged.

The drum beats continued: 'Is this going on all night?' she clutched Ronnie's hand.

He made his 'pshaw' noise. 'Those are real Sussi talking drums. Didn't you want one? You like African junk.'

He was right. But in her bedroom in the capital, the raffia mats, the statues, the wooden bowls held none of this menacing presence. The drumming continued. Muriel slammed the window shut and turned the ceiling fan up to Full.

The boy who'd served beer, who looked oddly like Ezeh in spite of his yellow complexion announced: 'Dinner t'irty minnit, sah.'

Ezeh was waiting at the bottom of the curving wooden staircase. He wore a red and green-striped bou-bou with gold embroidery around the neck and hem. Muriel thought he should have worn a suit. He ushered them into a dining room with peeling ochre paint and flickering geckos clustering on the ceiling. Drums, instead of statues, lined the walls: small, hand-held drums; tall, narrow drums; short, squat drums; heavy, ceremonial drums bound with leather strips, and decorated with blue beads and cowry shells.

The yellow boy served, helped by a young girl, wearing a tiger-printed lappa twisted high round her chest, dozens of tiny plaits sticking out of her head at right angles.

'Ronnie, must take a photo first thing tomorrow,' whispered Muriel.

The girl, her palms outstretched beneath a steel bowl containing stew, knelt in turn to each guest; first Muriel, then Ronald, then Samuel, who had arrived from the Government Rest House with his terylene suit neatly pressed. When the girl reached Ezeh's chair, he flipped down the edge of her lappa and flicked his forefinger against her nipple, at which she giggled and continued serving. Each time the small brown breast bounced past, Ronald's eyes bulged like a goldfish expecting a food drop.

'Dis make too much pepper for you, Madam Ronald? Cook, 'e no savvy whiteman's chop.'

'No, no, not at all. Not frightfully hungry, you know.' The stew, four cows' feet, horn and bristles still on, poking above a viscous, red sauce, made her nauseous. 'No, not hungry at all.'

Urging Ronald to another helping of cassava, the colour and consistency of wet cement, Ezeh grinned until his lips split like overripe figs. 'Oh, my wife, how she loves dis stuff.'

What stuff − the pot of cassava or the bowl of jasmine, its sickly scent conflicting with the pungent palm-oil? Muriel's eyebrow twitched. 'Your wife... ?'

'She stay in England, Madam, for 'er work.'

'Doesn't your wife work here?'

'Oh, no, Madam. She teacher.'

'Why that's wonderful. Why Ronald's always saying you need more teachers.'

Ezeh lifted first one shoulder then the other, reversed the gesture, then turned towards Ronald: 'And what time tomorrow, Mr Marchant, would you care to commence? Will nine o'clock in my office be convenient?'

Ezeh's slithers between Pidgin and standard English puzzled and destabilised Muriel. She said, 'Why can't she teach in N'wekepiti?'

'Who is she?' said Ezeh.

'Your wife, of course.'

'No job 'ere.' Tipping back his chair, he twisted sideways and beat a rat-a-tat-tat on a large drum. 'My wife Philosophy teacher. She and I students togedder. We meet in Oxford.'

Ronald, who'd read Economics at Leeds Poly, whispered behind his hand: 'Never fire until you see the whites of their eyes. Too much pepper indeed! Just let Mister Ezeh wait!' Muriel kicked his ankle. 'Oh, steady on,' cried Ronald.

Ezeh ushered them into another lofty room. In here, the statues were ranked in rows two or three deep. Muriel kept trying not to stare at several phalluses.

'Never like them around me while I eat. Discouraging for appetite but good for conversation, don't you think?' Ezeh patted the smooth flank of an two-thirds life-size woman.

Muriel had never seen anything less encouraging for either. Some people considered this primitive stuff highly artistic; she found it obscene.

The young girl knelt, on her flattened palms rested a wooden bowl heaped with kola nuts. Samuel stretched out an eager hand, caught Ronald's eye and waved the girl away.

Ezeh, crunching a large kola nut, chewed and chewed, talked and talked: 'Rural development is what we need – especially in our regions. Greater autonomy here – that is what I'm asking for. Too much power centralised in the capital will be Africa's ruin. I wish it won't be so. You will see. Your poet has said it – the centre cannot hold.' A red stream of kola juice aimed towards the spittoon, fell short. Judging from dried orange smears on the floor, it had happened before.

Ronald shifted from one buttock to the other, always a sign of unease. By the time Ezeh had explained the necessity of subsidising indigenous culture and the benefits of daily tots of palm-wine for a healthy urinary-genital tract, her own attention had wandered to the crawk-crawk of frogs coming the lagoon, and the clack of crickets. The breeze kept away mosquitoes and the rotting fish smell. What was the woman with the pots doing at this moment? Slipping off her shoes, she doubled her legs under her. Ezeh's voice swayed and boomed. Pacing up and down, waving his cheroot, he, too, had taken off his sandals and his flexible big toe humped along like a caterpillar.

'As you are doing, Samuel, I started work in our magnificent capital, What a waste of time. My Minister – I would ask myself – of which did he have greater number – wives or Swiss bank accounts?' Ezeh grinned at Samuel's barely suppressed gasp. 'Ah, Samuel, you don't like me to mention such matters before important guests. These are grave matters. They must not be hidden. They drove me back to the bush. Here, I have all I need. Here, I do as I please.' One hand slapped his chest and he bowed, 'Except of course, when your goodselves arrive on inspection visit.'

Ronald hurrumphed. 'Backward regions like this one need progress.'

'Ah, progress, progre-ss-ss.' Ezeh lingered on the word as though he were tasting it. 'Delicious! But what does it mean? For you, Mr Marchant, a swelling administration. More filing cabinets and clerks to fill them up. And regulations. Ah, yes. More of those . Everyone needs more of those. I, myself, am very fond of the double entry. For Samuel, – what for him? Let him indulge in a brand new airport with national colours painted on the tails of large airplanes. For me – the choice is easy – a patch of cassava in the bush and a chicken scratching in the dirt.' He leant both hands on the arms of Muriel's chair and bent forwards: 'And what for you, Mrs Ronald?'

With his face held an inch from hers and the smell of palm oil on his breath, she stammered... cheap housing perhaps... Ronnie always insisting that primary schooling was...

Ezeh grinned, seeming delighted with these flabby answers. 'Now comes time for rest. In the morning there is work to do. I wish that you sleep well, my friends.

Hand-in-hand like children being sent to bed, Muriel and Ronald mounted the curving staircase. In delicate white folds, the mosquito net floated down from the ceiling; many fat pillows were heaped high; blue-white sheets crackled with starch on a high, brass-railed bed.

Ronald stretched and yawned, 'Quite the bridal chamber! Corruption in high places indeed! Let's see what turns up here. These brainy blokes aren't trustworthy. Fine good idea of my minister to ship him out East and let him preach his radical ideas to bushmen. Wouldn't be surprised if he turns out to be a communist. Well, g'night, m'dear.'

Muriel's thoughts churned. In some obscure fashion she felt they'd been made fun of. Her stomach rumbled; stupid of her not to have packed some Marie biscuits. Could she buy some tomorrow? She sensed the statues' presence. Were they watching? Too dark to tell. A beam of light caught a crack in the ceiling: one moment it looked like a river; then it became a crack again. Ripples of distant laughter. Why were all the children Ezeh look-alikes? A sickly-sweet smell seeped up from the floorboards... jasmine mixed with... her nostrils twitched... rotting fish?

*

Ronald, finishing a hearty English breakfast, toast, two fried eggs and fatty bacon (in case Ezeh got up to his culinary tricks again at lunch) asked: 'Think you'll be alright, old girl, on your own?'

'On her own!' Ezeh's tone was light, 'with thirty-eight people living on the compound?'

'Not quite what I meant, old chap.'

'Ah,' said Ezeh and flashed his teeth.

'No problem, I'll walk along with you,' said Muriel, remembering her Marie biscuits.

Samuel arrived at nine o'clock precisely and they set off for the D.O.s office. Muriel regretted her nylons sticking her thighs together. They came apart at each step with a discreet squelch that she hoped no one could hear. Ezeh's sandals slapped on the broken concrete slabs of the quayside. A little boy beat a tam-tam and a dozen children, in a multi-coloured, raggedy tail, capered behind their four-person procession. Ezeh remarked: 'Big People – all gone live Upper Town – only me left down here.'

They reached the end of the quay. Outside the Old Customs House, scarlet and yellow Canna lilies grew in rusty kerosene cans, ringlets of peeling cream paint curled down the walls. On the wide, shallow veranda steps, a crowd of fishermen, villagers and market women, chewed kola nuts. Ronald and Samuel, eyes ahead, filed past, their attaché cases displaying the gold-embossed Government crest. Ronald, Muriel noted with regret, didn't cut as impressive a figure as she hoped; the Africans kept up their noise in a shocking show of disrespect. Real Africa wasn't turning out quite what she had expected.

'I'll take photos,' she called, waving goodbye. She concentrated on the picture postcard aspect of the scene; cormorants diving in the lagoon, their snake-like heads swaying above their black feathers and fleets of canoes plying the palm-lined waterways. A golden disk blazed in a furiously blue sky. After half-an-hour, these exotic sights palled as the smell of rotting fish grew stronger and wherever she walked, a gaggle of giggling barefoot children followed, waggling their arms. She wheeled round, the children froze. 'Go away. Go away. Leave me alone,' she snapped, 'I'm not the Pied Piper.'

'Pie-pipa, pie-pipa,' trilled the children, backing off a few paces before returning like flies settling over a gutted fish.

Back in her room, the ceiling fan whirred, the statues leered and one of her headaches throbbed. At one o'clock the Ezeh-like boy brought up a tray containing an omelette, a glass of wine and a spray of jasmine in a blue vase. When Ronald arrived half an hour later, she thanked him.

'Don't thank me – not my doing – must be Ezeh. We've just been subjected to another of his culinary jokes. Today's had chicken, meat and fish boiled up together. Not funny! Heads on, too! Ezeh called it Bitterleaf Soup. He'll be eatin' bitter leaf before we're through.' And marching back and forth in a gap between two statues, rubbing his hands, cock-a-hoop with success, he gave an account of his morning's work. The files had yielded their secrets on first examination. 'After I'd explained to Samuel how the trick was done, he caught on straightaway. Doesn't make a bad Watson.'

'A Watson?'

'To my Sherlock Holmes, you duffer. Simple, m'boy, I told him – once you've rumbled the wheeze. Ezeh thinks he's a smart-aleck. So smart, he's hardly bothered to cover his tracks.'

Her headache came back; she didn't want to hear. With an effort she said, 'So what have you found out?' Ronald explained: Government census listed the number of men eligible for poll; Ezeh's returns for the district differed slightly from the official figures, a few heads were missing from each village, never more than six or eight but – and this was the all-important but – when you added them all up, nearly six hundred pounds were unaccounted for. 'It's a bloody small fortune,' Ronald huffed. Had Ezeh kept the money or split the profit with the village headmen? In all probability no one would ever know. The money had vanished.

'Quite so.' And she sighed. What had appeared so necessary in the capital – checking on the cook's marketing, searching for purloined eggs in the garden boy's room, marking the level in the whisky bottles – the whole effort of rooting out corruption before all of them all had to go Home – hardly seemed to matter down here. Ronald's oh, so important discoveries were diminished. Peals of laughter floated up from the compound. What were they laughing at? And again she sighed.

Ronald hated hearing her sigh. 'You see. Overtired. Didn't I tell you not to come? Outstations aren't suitable for a white woman even nowadays.'

'Oh, Ronnie don't be so stuffy! It's 1958 – not 1858!'

That night at dinner, Ezeh must have given the cook different instructions. The pepper quantity had diminished and Muriel found herself almost enjoying the stew – river fish with a smoky flavour. Next to a calabash of palm-wine, a green bottle poked its cheerful, stubby stubby neck out of a wicker basket.

'Oh, Beaujolais, what fun! We never seem to find a drop in the capital.'

'I trust a Government officer,' Ronald's thumb and forefinger flattened his mustache, 'never stoops to acquire smuggled goods.'

'Stooping? No need, Ronald.' Ezeh chuckled. 'A good vintage. A good year!'

Samuel fingered the knot in his tie, opened his mouth, then shut it.

Muriel sipped – extraordinarily good. 'Why are you laughing, Ezeh?'

'Ah, Mrs Ronald, we blackmen always laughing. Come. Onto your feet. Time. It is time. This evening, I take you to the Olympia.'

Muriel raised an eyebrow and slightly cocked her head. But Ronald ignored her signal, almost as if, and this was ridiculous, Ezeh, not he, was in charge. Samuel was holding the door open. There was nothing left for her but acquiescence. Out she marched, head up, with an image of intrepid lady explorers like Mary Kingsley sustaining her annoyance.

*

Mud-walled shacks, their tin roofs striped red, green and orange from the reflected glow of the night-club's neon lights, huddled against the Olympia's perimeter wall. Palm trees swayed with boys in bunches clinging below their crowns; inside the open-air enclosure, town spivs propped themselves up on high stools, fists full of beer bottles, admiring their pointed shoes and clicking their fingers at big-bottomed girls strutting to and fro.

'What's that funny smell – like incense?' asked Muriel.

'Ah,' Ezeh steered her quickly past a group of youths sharing an outsize, hand-rolled cigarette, 'life is composed of funny smells.'

At the sight of Ezeh, customers stamped their feet and waved bottles of beer. He gave a clenched fist salute.

Under the bright lights, Samuel perked up. Ronald boomed: 'Now, Muriel, a rather interesting habit to observe...'

'Oh, do let's sit down.' She feared a lecture on native customs. They were conspicuous enough without Ronald imparting information to everyone within earshot.

Swags of red, green and yellow light bulbs swayed above the platform on which a semi-circle of eight musicians banged, thumped and blew.

'Shall we dance, Mrs Marchant?' Ezeh stood up. He was half-a head shorter.

'Oh, no, no. Never tried this sort of thing. Never.'

'No matter.'

She hesitated; Ronald was calling for drinks, Samuel tapping his foot and drumming on the table with his knuckles. Well, why not? Real Africa was what she'd come for. She let Ezeh lead her down two steps. He held her loosely amongst writhing coils of dancers, attached to one another by invisible strings. Each couple swayed lower and lower, their gyrating bottoms oscillating up, down and sideways. So embarrassing! A duet started between the lead singer and drummer and the dancers snapped their invisible strings and formed a trudging circle, isolating Muriel and Ezeh in the centre.

'What's he singing?'

'White lady she come N'wekepiti. Her man big man. She sit on her hair.'

'He can't know how long my hair is.'

'Why not? You in Africa now, Mrs Ronald.'

She tried to sway her hips as she'd seen the other women do. She couldn't do it; they only jerked. The clapping grew louder and faster.

'Now what's it about?'

'No matter. He sings about me.'

Customers jumped up onto the platform to stick coins onto the singer's forehead. Beads of sweat acted like glue. When several coins had stuck, he shook his head, letting the money fall into his cupped palms. Ronald pasted a pound note across the singer's forehead. Ezeh immediately released Muriel and stuck two notes crossways. Bending forward with one fluid gesture, the singer peeled off them off without missing a beat.

'Can we sit down, please?'

In the safety of the Ronnie's presence, her tense neck muscles relaxed. For a moment, in that mêlée of gleaming bodies, a crazy desire had surfaced, to untie her hair, throw it over her face and lead the others in a conga out of the snake pit and through the town.

'So. You like Highlife, Mrs Ronald?' Ezeh grinned as if he'd read her thoughts. 'The Olympia gives satisfaction, yes? I think you never hear such drums before?'

'Perhaps not.' She drew deeply on her cigarette and coughed. Samuel Odekunjo had winked at that fat barmaid. Aren't men disgusting! The young girl serving their drinks looked like her younger sister. A pretty little thing. How sad she had to work in a bar.

From an adjoining table, littered with beer and two whisky bottles, two sinewy young women, wearing elaborate satin turbans, one pink, the other orange, stood up to dance, partnered by a pair of red-faced men.

'Extraordinary,' Muriel remarked, 'like flamingos with lobsters, aren't they?'

'Indeed so,' Ezeh replied. 'They must have come up from the capital. They enjoy better earnings up here – less competition.'

Muriel's lips tightened. 'You mean they're... ?' The apricot-coloured girls swayed back to their table, gold earrings swinging against slender necks.

'Ex-pen-sive,' Samuel murmured.

Ronald patted her knee. 'Won't do you any harm, m'dear, seeing a bit of life in the raw.' And beckoning the little waitress, he said, 'My round. Same again gentlemen – Muriel?'

'Nothing. Absolutely nothing.' She sat up straight. 'Ronald, can we go? Such a noise!'

'What did you expect? The Torquay Palais de Danse?'

'My headache's come back again.'

Ronald usually took ladies' headaches (hers especially) seriously. Not tonight however. 'Oh, what a shame! We've only just arrived. Not had a dance with you yet. Not that it's my style, what! He wobbled upright. 'Let's show the flag. Give it a damned good try, shall we?'

'I don't want a try. I want to go!'

Ezeh gently pressed Ronald's arm. Ronald subsided into his chair. 'Let me take Mrs Ronald home, Mr Marchant.'

Ronald started to protest, then changed his mind: 'Oh, all right. Go on ahead, Muriel. I'll be along shortly.'

Without making a scene, there's nothing she can do. As she brushes past their table, the apricot girls twitch the corners of their shapely mouths, making Muriel conscious of her sweaty hair plastered to her neck.

*

The Humber provides a refuge, comforting in its luxury. Why hasn't Ronnie come, dam him? She wedges herself into the corner, as the car, bumping over the unpaved roads, throws her and Ezeh against one another. King Kong's understudy, that's what he is, she tells herself – and he smells.

'My wife – she doesn't care for Highlife.'

'Really?'

'Piano music she prefers – Chopin.'

'How interesting! Does she play?'

'Why d'you ask?'

'Well, I don't know – it seems funny...'

'Ah, you suppose she cannot play the piano?'

'Of course not!'

'Must she be a white goddess and sit on her hair – before she can?'

The dark hides Muriel's blush. 'I-I'm sorry. I didn't mean to sound... '

'Oh, Muriel! Can't you start finding people – instead of servants?'

'Oh, that is unfair. I have African friends. I really do.'

'You really do. Rahly,' he mocks. 'People you're so frightf'ly polite to at cocktail parties and Polo matches and make fun of when they leave. African friends? Black friends? Friends with woolly hair? Friends like me?' His voice drops to its normal bass. 'Not so, my dear Muriel, indubitably not so.'

'What I meant... what I mean... Well, not exactly. I'm broad-minded. I collect art. I've got cupboards full. Why, ask Ronald. He'll tell you I came East to find... '

'To find? Stop your absurd words. A squawking chicken makes more sense. No matter'.

'I don't... '

'Don't you? Shall I tell you what you came to find?' His hands cup her shoulders, pushing her down until their eyes are level. Her hips slide forward and her eyes close. His mouth covers hers, and with a will of its own, her tongue slips between his soft, dry lips. The car stops. Opening her eyes, she sees the woolly, inert driver's head. Ezeh leans across and opens the car door.

In the bathroom, she gargles, brushing her teeth until her gums bleed. If only those beastly drums would shut up. In the mirror, the blind eyes of the bronze mask gleam. A shadow darkens the mirror.

'What're you doing up here? What're you... ?'

The toothbrush drops onto the tiled floor. Her hand stretches out – stilled in its downward motion.

Without a word, Ezeh, taking hold of her empty hand, leads her, blind-eyed as the bronze mask, up and onto the mosquito-netted, bridal bed.

*

With her pink cotton skirt stretched so tight across her bottom, Ronald sees that the little waitress has no knickers on. Saliva fills his mouth. He runs a finger round his too-tight collar. From behind the bar, the barmaid gives a nod and the younger girl inserts herself into Muriel's empty chair.

'Good evening, Sah, I am Ismelda.'

Ronald flushes. What's he supposed to do? Even if he wants to (and he doesn't) he couldn't possibly in front of Samuel. He's never behaved like some of the fellows – never gone with native girls. The little strumpet keeps eyeing the bar, her hand curled up on his thigh like an unwanted kitten. He looks around; no one's taking any notice. Why she's hardly older than Nancy, his own daughter. She ought to be in bed; she ought to be punished for staying up so late. He finds himself squeezing her wrist.

The Master calls the class to attention. 'Ismelda, you've been a very bad, naughty girl. You must and shall be punished. Bend over. Lower. Pull down your panties. Right down. And you, other bad girls. Do it too. All bend over.' Thwack! Thwack! The girls squeal. 'Ismelda, beg my pardon.'

'Suh, please, Suh, you hurt me.'

Ronald releases his grasp and drains his beer glass. Samuel beckons. The fat barmaid ducks under the bar-flap and sways, broadhipped, towards them. Samuel says in a matter-of-fact voice, 'Ezeh won't be coming back, Sir.'

The speed of events fuddles Ronald. At nine o'clock, he's been sitting beside Muriel, watching some jolly fine natives disport themselves in jolly native fashion. At ten o'clock, he's begun to behave like one himself. Not so jolly. This has to be Muriel's fault. Why the hell did she rush off like that? He recalls his most recent attempt at lovemaking – last Saturday night, wasn't it? Another of her blasted, neurotic headaches.

'Time for us to be getting along, what?' He flattens a pound note under the glasses and weaves towards the exit. The car has returned. Like a golden-green toad, it squats under the neon lights. Giggling and shoving, the sisters climb in on either side.

'What the deuce! Where'd they spring from? Get 'em out! We can't take 'em to Ezeh's.'

'So, so,' soothes Samuel, 'no, no. Let us just pop into the Rest House for a night-cap, no?'

Ronald wants to lean forward to instruct the driver to drop him off first but he cannot free himself from Ismelda, who has stopped giggling and lies half in his lap, light as a gull, waiting. Waiting? What for? His protection? He feels shame for the fantasy of having beaten her. He'll give her a present. He must get back, back to Muriel. In spite of the car's air-conditioning, his armpits sweat. He wipes his forehead. He's never slept with native girls – not like some of 'em. He has always believed in standards and said so. Must get back to Muriel... back to Muriel...

Without Ronald knowing how they got there, the four of them arrive in Samuel's room. Two mosquito-netted beds wallow like beached whales on the coconut-matted floor. Samuel's diffidence in front of his superior officer appears to have disappeared. He switches off the main lights, leaving the bathroom door ajar and turns on the radio. This game is one whose rules he has no problem understanding. As though offering a slice of cake at a mission tea-party, he asks, 'Would you care for take the bigger one, Sir?'

'N-no. Y-you go ahead. Go ahead.'

'Thanks, old man, thanks, ' replies Samuel. Light from the barred window stripes his girl's glossy rump turning her into a baby tigress; he gives an appreciative growl. Bayo is her name and her breasts are melons. No time wasted kissing; a couple of caresses and her firm thighs are hooked round his waist.

Ronald, sitting fully-dressed on the edge of the other bed, mosquito- net draped round his head and shoulders, watches a pair of see-sawing buttocks moving in time to Glen Miller. He sweats; he is afraid. The little girl, Ismelda, sits beside him. What must he do? Can she be a virgin? No, she can't be. The other bedhead knocks against the wall, as the other couple heave. A sharp rapping – rocking faster and faster. Bayo bucks like an unbroken filly. Unwilling for Samuel to realise that he's watching, Ronald pushes Ismelda under the net and grabs at her clothes. Her blouse and skirt come apart, uncovering a body (neither child nor woman) with little, pointy breasts – only a fluff of pubic hair. Nothing to catch hold of. He feels big, big and powerful.

'How old are you?'

'Suh, I am fourteen years, Suh.'

Either she's lying or doesn't know her real age. How can she be more than twelve? But she knows what she's doing – it can't be the first time. Or can it? When he tries to kiss her lips she turns her head and his mouth slides over to her ear. Nor can his swollen prick find the way into her tight little pussy. She clasps her hands, forming a bowl over her belly. At this, his erection subsides. The rhythmic knock knock of the bedhead opposite grows louder and faster. A climax is approaching – but elsewhere. Ronald licks Ismelda's flat nipples. Beneath his tongue, they stiffen. His erection returns at the sight of the little purple bulbs. He attempts again, digging his nails into her arms, growing rougher with each failure. Finally, he falls limp on top of her, his face buried in the pillow.

The lavatory flushes. Samuel returning, on seeing the two-backed beast stationary, gives Bayo a little push. 'Why not try this one for size, old man?'

Ronald, brimful of lust and remorse, cannot even reply to this vulgar request. Ismelda slides out from beneath him and Bayo wriggles in under the net. He wants to cry out to Samuel. He wants him to send Ismelda back. Not wanting to look, but unable to look elsewhere, he sees Samuel straddle her and start rocking up and down.

Bayo freshly washed, pushes against his thigh and shoulder until he rolls over onto his back. 'Sorry, Suh. You no want me. You no want my sister. OK, I do what whitelady do.'

Bending over his belly, she sucks Ronald's limp prick, kneading his buttocks and thighs with firm, experienced fingers. 'You like? English roadman – he show me how.' Bending over him again, she sucks and sucks, pressing, squeezing, almost gagging until he comes with a wheezing moan. She spits, wipes her mouth, giggles and jumps off the bed.

*

Muriel doesn't stir when, later, much later, he climbs up onto the high, brass-railed bed. He falls asleep with his back to her. During the night, he must have changed position for they wake up wrapped in each other's arms, something which they've not done for years. At breakfast, refusing his offer of buttered toast, Muriel drinks her coffee black, her eyes mauve-shadowed, her face puffy. That headache must have been genuine. He doesn't feel too sparky himself.

'Took a drop too much last night, Ezeh. I shall walk to the office to clear m'head, Odekunjo should be waiting already over there. Investigation's complete. I'd like to wind up and be off before luncheon, what.'

If Ronald expected Ezeh to show some anxiety, he has to be disappointed. Ezeh pours more coffee for himself and Muriel and waves a casual arm. 'See you later, old man.'

Alone with Ezeh, Muriel can't think of what to talk about and he's no help, tipping his chair back on two legs and puffing his blasted cheroot. What subject is neutral? Weather? Trite. The Olympia? No! Ezeh, it seems, can sit at ease without saying a word. Several children shuffle into the room, giggling and one boy twitches the hem of her dress. She grabs it away.

'Go play,' says Ezeh. The children vanish.

'Whose children are they, anyway?'

'Some – mine. Some are homeless. That little waitress at the Olympia, Ismelda, she's mine. Her Ma ran off with a Northerner, so I look after her.' His fingers snap. 'Must find her a husband. And soon. She'll be hot, too hot – like her mother and sister.'

Irritation sharpens Muriel's voice: 'D'you enjoy arranging people's lives?'

'Enjoy? How else shall I behave? I am chief here. My grandfather, he was Paramount Chief before you people took away his powers.'

Beneath the veranda, a fisherman hails a greeting. Ezeh leans over the rails and drops coins into the man's boat. Muriel's irritation deepens; she will not give in. Give-in? What to? Shall she warn Ezeh? Crazy ideas zigzag through her mind. Could she stay in N'wekepiti? Help him? That progress and development he wants – couldn't she be useful? In spite of herself, she feels the creamy edge of desire, softening, warm and secret with a smell of jasmine, a smell of Ezeh. Damn him!

'Don't worry, Muriel.' Taking both hands, he pulls her onto her feet, 'It is not important.'

He's wrong but she cannot, in face of that enigmatic smile, tell him what is important.

'I need little. A clearing in the jungle. Can't you see – I already have one? So back to your capital, my dear. And your art. Your oh-so-precious African art.'

Her fingers are layered between his dry palms. What's left to say? She wants, oh, she wants to kiss him. Tears tickle the back of her nose like a sneeze, as, politely, but inexorably, before they can fall, he steers her backwards into the hallway. She climbs the wooden stairs, step by step, hoping to hear him call her name, hoping to be recalled. No call comes.

In the statue-filled bedroom, last night's bed is dreamless, already remade, the sheets virgin white, the pillows uncreased. At last, the talking-drums have fallen silent. The fan languidly turns. Folding Ronald's crumpled clothes into the bottom of his suitcase, her knuckles scrape against something hard – an object wrapped in a fringed cloth. Unwrapping it, she holds up the blind-eyed, bronze mask. And at last, she understands its smile.

*

When Ronald, sallow and hungover, arrives in the District Officer's office, he finds Samuel, white-shirted and shaved, flirting with Ezeh's secretary. The crowd of Africans, larger than the day before, are making a din.

'More quiet out there,' Ronald bawls.

'Certainly, Suh,' agrees the secretary, prancing onto the veranda. The noise hushes for a few minutes and then starts up. Ronald strides up and down the office, furious that he is having to wait for Ezeh, who shows up at ten o'clock. Ronald hands over the poll tax returns with a certain flourish. Ezeh scans the columns of figures, studying the sheet attentively. A row of question marks, boldly scored with Ronald's red crayon, appears to amuse him.

'Irregularity? Mr Marchant, Suh? Surely irregularity, lies in the eye of the beholder – like beauty, too – you know?'

Ronald splutters – excuses are not going to be accepted – D.O.'s responsibility to central government – indictable offences...

Ezeh's laughter shakes his shoulders. 'You've examined my reports; my district is best run in the region. Best run in the whole country – probably.'

'That's as may be. At close scrutiny your figures don't stand up. They collapse!' Ronald's hangover beats an uneven tattoo against his temples. 'Wait, you just wait until the Minister has been told. You'll face dismissal... maybe worse... '

'Mr Marchant, my dear friend, you will not tell the Minister, who, incidentally... ' Ezeh thumbs an imaginary roll of bank notes. 'Ah, no, Mr Marchant, surely no longwinded investigations into your stay in N'wekepiti,' his arms stretch high above his head and his jaws rotate in a yawn, 'regrettably short though it has been.'The yawn stops with a click of teeth. 'Your white Madonna - now take her home quickly - or else!'

'Or else - or else what! What the hell are you getting at?'

Ezeh's hand covers his mouth too late to hide his creeping smile.'Ah no, you wouldn't want...you couldn't afford...'

'Want? Afford? Trying a spot of blackmail now are you?'

'Ronnie, please,please forgive.' Ezeh's smile shines forth. 'Oh, forgive me, you must.Awful puns.I could never resist. No, not blackmail you .Only Whitemale!.

His eyes roll with amusement at his own feeble joke.Ronald stares: They are like....exactly like....Ah no, it can not - can not possibly be? Ronald's flush leaves his face pale.In the draughty room, he shivers.Slowly, the report slides back into the gold-embossed attache case. His own daughter? His own? And Muriel? Muriel, hollow-eye, silent at breakfast. What had Ezeh said? White Madonna? Jasmine? A cockroach, its claws tapping out the unthinkable, scutters across the linoleum of Ronald's mind.

Ismelda, my little dream, where are you?

His attaché case clicks shut. 'My report *will* be presented, don't you think otherwise.'

Ezeh tips his chair back onto two legs, winks at Samuel and relights his cheroot.

*

The Marchants clamber into the Humber's back seat. On this return journey Ronald makes no move to encourage Samuel to join them.

'The Minister'll be ever so pleased,' Samuel stretched an arm across the front seat , because he hates these university chaps.D'you think Ezeh will be charged , Mr Marchant, Sir?'

'Charged? What ever for old man? Ezeh's district's best run in the region - probably the whole country - you said yourself.'

'I did?' Samuel's Old School tie presses against his Adam's apple; he yanks it off, squashes it into his pocket.

'Yes, of course you did. Census figures are notorious for being out of date. Best leave well alone. Irregularity's in the eye of the beholder. Like beauty, too, y'know. You can quote me, what!'

Through the driving mirror, Samuel observes that Ronald has taken Muriel's hand and covered it with his own. They sit bolt upright side by side, eyes straight ahead. He can almost see Union Jacks reflected in their eyeballs. Muriel's brown canvas hat flops over her forehead. He might have understood had she been pretty. He might have understood if money had changed hands. But white men don't take bribes. Or do they? He accepts defeat. He is only a spectator. Once again the ball-players are playing the game to some rule that he has not mastered. And will he ever? He doubts it.

No, Samuel never mastered the rules but that did not prevent him ending up Permanent Secretary in Ronald's old ministry. Poor old Ronnie. His report was handed in too close to Independence. Probably no one ever read it. Ronald ended up selling second hand cars in Chelmsford. He and Muriel are still together. Retired now of course. Ismelda is manageress of the Olympia, renamed Independence Hall.

And Ezeh?

He was shot in the civil war a couple of years later.

-oOo-

Separate and Together

My mother doesn't bother to ask who's looking after Paulie – now that I'm in here all day looking after her. Mum looks rather like a baby herself now – a shrunken one with cotton wool hair. Most of it's fallen out but what's left is fluffy and Shireen, the Jamaican nurse, brushes it every morning.

Mum won't stop fidgeting, sticking her fingers in the mohair shawl I bought her from Spain. And Shireen tries to stop her. Like my father used to. Like he wouldn't let her bite her nails; they were her nails – not his! Funny to think of him stuck with Suzanne after twenty-seven years with Mum – ending up in a two-room flat in Weymouth. Will he get here on time? Do I want him anyway? It's her that I'm filming. I've got this idea for something mindblowing, totally original. Something no one has ever dared film before.

God, I'm tired. I've been stuck in this hospice since ten this morning and I need a cigarette. She keeps repeating that she's in here for convalescence. I hope no one tells her the truth. This is no rehearsal; this is the real thing.

Yesterday she became quite lively: 'D'you remember that set of Russian dolls? The ones I gave you for Christmas – the year before your father pissed off. One doll fitting inside the other, down to the littlest one. A whole row of dollies.'

I didn't reply. But I remembered. She didn't give them to me. We all wanted them but Tom got them. Tom always had first pick. Because he's the eldest – Mum would say.

Mum used her 'little-me' voice: 'I so loved the way each doll fitted – one inside another – separate and together. That's a problem. It always has been, hasn't it?'

I've never bought her, 'What's the meaning-of-life?' stuff; it just confuses issues. Just words, never the thoughts beneath. Don't like sentimental mush. I never have. That's not the idea. What's it like to die – that's the idea. I showed what it was like to be born. I held the camera while I gave birth to Paulie. Anything can be filmed – if you're brave enough and keep your hands steady.

Such tight lips the staff have when I arrive each morning. They think I'm hardboiled. I'm not – just realistic. Filming's my job – like nursing's theirs. They can't see that.

Mum's always been self-centred: 'Everything I've ever done has been for your good,' her eternal catchphrase. She probably believes it. But she never thought of me after Dad left. 'You can't share my flat,' I told her, 'it's too small.' That didn't mean she had to go off in a huff to a cottage in the back-of-beyond and never be around to babysit.

When I asked her why, she didn't answer and started fussing about the cat. Who's looking after it? The cat's fine, I assured her, the cat's fine. Little lies can't hurt at this stage. The cat disappeared two days after we brought her here. I think a local farmer shot it.

I film my mother, her body lying on this bed.

If only the camera could pass through the shut eyes and focus on what's happening under those bruised eyelids? If only I could ask the right questions.

I keep the camera running but she falls asleep again and wakes up with unfocussed eyes, mumbling about houses. What house does she mean? That pretentious cottage with fake beams that she's so proud of, or that monstrosity in Richmond where we grew up.

Shireen brings in the post.

'Open it, Sara. Oh, do open it,' Mum says. 'That's your father's writing.'

An enormous card smothered in glitter – Suzanne must have picked that.

'"Get Well." Isn't that nice? Oh, yes, I shall. I'll soon be out of here and back home, won't I? Oh, do stop filming, Sara.'

'Shush, Mother. Rest.'

I pin Dad's card up on the wall; there aren't many.

'You and Dad should never have bought that house?' When I say that she sucks in her bottom lip. Her favourite family myth concerns our happy, happy childhood. What a joke! Her and Dad quarrelling behind double doors in that falling-down mansion. And there were rats in the cellar. Who were they trying to fool? They couldn't afford it.

One thing made her proud, she whispers: 'Such a happy childhood I gave you, didn't I?'

What can I answer?

I tuck her chilly hands under the sheets and say I'll be back in the morning. It's tempting to leave the camera running all night. She's either asleep or pretending. She agreed to make the film and now she won't cooperate.

When I nod good night to the receptionist, she gives me that funny look, which, I suppose, is to be expected – doing what I'm doing.

Mum's getting weaker. The staff keep hinting that filming's too strenuous. I shan't take any notice unless they chuck me out. Goldberg's waiting like a spider in that office. He says the film can't be done. Got to prove him wrong. Breaking the last taboo – Death. Not many filmakers would dare. I dare.

I want to make her talk about the past but truthfully – not the myths she surrounds herself with. She's so reluctant – like she was ashamed – like she kept guilty secrets. What can she be ashamed of? She's never done anything. Tom said when he was small: 'Daddy's an office gentleman. Mummy's a shopping lady.'

She isn't making much sense. Who's she talking about?

'Where are they?' she keeps asking. 'I want him.' Who's the him? Is that the secret? I won't believe there are any. I tell her that my brothers aren't here yet. They're on their way. It's not true. I doubt that they'll arrive before the end. They say they're terribly busy. So am I. It would be me – left picking up the pieces. Good old Sara.

Where is Dad?

Why isn't he here? I phoned: how's your mother, recovering alright? Suzanne sends love; we're off to Corfu next week – a spot of sailing.

He'll neither understand, nor face it. Won't he just have to – when he sees the film. He used to say he couldn't stand that fidgeting she does. I don't blame him. She won't stop picking – trying to find a single thread which holds the shawl together. There isn't one.

She says: 'Your father got on so well with my family. In spite of all the differences.' Her smile pleads; my jaws ache. 'Your father's always been a tolerant man.' And who's she kidding? She pretended for years her family was something special. They were just refugees.

Shireen's toothpaste ad smile overrides mine. Mum's crazy about this nurse.

More light. I must have more light. So far I've got some super shots. The slow decay, the way the body slips its moorings and the mind skids and skates over reality. For a second, under the dim ceiling light, a girl surfaces from beneath the bones. Then Shireen flicks on the bedside light and the girl sinks beneath Mum's grey face. I should be filming this. Mum's thighs appear quite lanky – almost girlish – in spite of her wasted muscles. Then the gown slips – a few scanty tufts of grey. Oh, no, I can't film this! I can't! I've dropped my camera! Oh, my God! Today she doesn't recognise me. That officious Shireen draws the curtains round the bed, shutting me out. I wait... wondering when I'm going to be able to film. Whatever's happening is happening behind the curtain.

I pull open the curtain a few inches. 'Mum, wake up. You've been dozing all day.'

'Leave her in peace, Sara.'

'Don't you tell me what to do, Shireen. She's my mother.' I've put hothouse grapes on the bedside table, expensive ones. 'Mum... ?' She won't respond. I haven't filmed enough, not nearly enough. I don't seem to... there's no... I can't...

The film isn't important. Not anymore.

This is my mother and she's dying.

I yank the curtains apart; they squeal on their runners. I pick up the camera. She just lies there. Oh, God, make her speak! Make her speak, God. This is hopeless. She's humming, Hickory, Dickory, Dock. Oh, no! That's what she used to sing to us. Her fingers are trapped, wrapped around with woollen threads, so tight they've gone blue. A snarl of mauve and pink. And it cost ten thousand pesetas.

Shireen brings in a vase of lilies and says, 'Uh-uh! Your Papa and brothers never come. Pity that. She wanted to see them. You pleased with your film?' As if she cared.

'It's gonna be great!'

I'm lying. Don't give a damn about the bloody film. There isn't enough. Not nearly enough. Nothing significant. Goldberg was right. You can't film somebody's death. Not when they're dying. We could've talked properly. Maybe I could've, I could've told her... that I, that I... that – I loved her.

Shireen cuts the threads with surgical scissors; they scatter on the floor. She takes my mother's wrist and feels for her pulse. 'Not long now.' Her features click into an appropriate expression.

Damn the rules, I'm going to smoke. Fuck! My cigarette packet's empty.

The grapes are untouched; the shawl's ruined.

What a waste!

-oOo-

The Sound
of
Silence

(for Geshe Thupten Jinpa)

M y name is Heather Dodrington and I am (or was) a missionary.
A calling which has lost its inner meaning in our present time.
As my short term memory falters, the past grows sharper like
the light that I watch every day intensify over the mountains. I first came
to this village in 1924. Do not imagine that the place is any Shangri-La
in spite of my great age. The secret of longevity that I have discovered
and documented is simple – extremely so: apricots (fresh and dried) live
yoghurt, the daily climbing of steep hills and a heart kept serene. These
last two are not easily found in that place from where, you, Mr Cox-
Williamson, have addressed your request. Your letter lies on my table
held flat by a lump of granite. I turn the granite over and over; it is
billions of years old. Whether I shall post these rambling notes in lieu of
a reply, I have not yet decided. Should the secret be shared or should it
die with me? No one remains with whom to share my predicament.

I am Heather Dodrington; I need to keep reminding myself of this.
The thoughts of the very old hover hither and thither like butterflies,
alighting for no apparent reason on one particular blossom rather than
another, retaining this detail but not that one.

When I arrived at the mission in 1925 or thereabouts, travelling for
three weeks from the Indian border, the mules walked (as they still do)
on the extreme edge of precipitous paths to avoid knocking their loads
against the rockface. A landslide had occurred only ten days before. In

the middle of the night, a fraction of mountain spur gave way with no warning and carved a path clean through the village. Twelve people dead. The timber of their houses tossed like matchsticks into the gorge below. I remember a black cooking pot dented on one side, dogs licking the spilt lentils. Where the houses had stood, huge boulders were strewn. The villagers call that mountain 'Giver of Life,' which seems as odd to me today as it did then. It was an inauspicious arrival, yet I have stayed and have spent more than seventy years (first working then waiting) here. My health remains remarkable. With the aid of a stick, I can still climb the flanks of the terraced hills, sit under the chorten and listen to the wind fluttering the strings of white prayer flags. From the half-ruined lamasery, I hear the blare of the thighbone trumpet and the beating of a gong. I look outwards, always North. That is the direction that Yerom took. The girl, who looks after me (Lo Hensing's granddaughter) clucks: 'Come indoors, Ama. Night comes. Spirits walk abroad.' I, who have nothing to fear and everything to wait and hope for, laugh at her fears.

Fewer and fewer people remain with whom I am in correspondence and a letter has recently arrived. It looks incongruous lying on my table, coming from another world. You sign yourself – David Cox-Williamson, Esquire. You write on cream paper with an embossed heading. From Miss Dodrington, should she still be alive, or if not, from anyone else, you request information; you claim that you are an aficionado of high mountains. Oh, I have known many such. You seek intelligence about an expedition which took place in October, 1936. The expedition was seeking the valley of Be-yul, which to this day has never been mapped. You would be grateful, etc. etc. Why should you want to know? Who is interested in those unfortunate explorers and why? Your curiosity, Mr Cox-Williamson, intrigues me. Yerom went upon a quest; only employees go on errands. Yerom's journey was not undertaken for material gain; he sought something unquantifiable. And what do you seek – the answer to a riddle? Your letter is suspiciously brief.

I am so old that I have the look of a tortoise. I am the last; none of the others are living. The lama, my dearest friend, died some ten years ago. Three elderly monks try to keep the ritual intact in the half-ruined lamasery. Their prayer wheels spin in the deserted chapels where the frescoes are peeling off the walls.

Now I live alone except for Lo Hensing's girl, who cooks a plate of rice and vegetables for me each evening and once a week boils up a caldron for my scanty needs of bath and laundry.

Years ago, life formed more elaborate patterns. Above us, the monastery resounded with the sonorous sound of many monks' chanting and below in the mission, we ourselves, Dr Martin, Helga, his wife, myself, our two helpers, Tsering and Joseph (our single convert), were active in many domains – the school, the clinic, my work on the dictionary. For simple declarative words like – body, head, heart or yak I found an Anglo-Saxon equivalent. Other words presented challenges. I picked familiar words from our hymn book: words like loving-kindness, pity, compassion. I could not find exact equivalents. Our village life used no such words. With time I have found some correspondence, although never sure I have transposed their inner meaning. Duty, honour, obedience – all our abstract concepts – in our village found expression in love and laughter and sympathy. My finished dictionary is unpublished. Perhaps, Mr Cox-Williamson, I should send you the manuscript? But let me not digress. You have asked for information.

The 1936 expedition, which set out to prove Be-yul's existence – that is the burden of your enquiry. Ah, yes, I know. And what I do not know I can imagine. I vouch neither for the veracity, nor the reality of my surmises for I have lived many years breathing thin air. My reactions are not those of a woman who lives at sea-level. Up here clarity breeds a sort of hallucination, which comes closer to truth. Everything exists much further off than it appears. The meaning of the mountains does not yield easily to the ridged confines of our language. Let me explain.

These mountains form the spine of the world and ancient glaciers and recent earthquakes form the valleys. In one such I live myself. I shall not tell you its name for you must not come here. You must not! We do not want the curious beating a path to our door. Beyond the head of the pass lie other valleys and yet more valleys, clefts within folds of mountains. How spidery my writing has become! Will you, Mr Cox-Williamson, be able to decipher it? When I have written, please desist from further enquiry.

The arrival of the children – that was the true Genesis of the expedition. Do not be impatient with what seems an old woman's circumlocutions. To grasp Be-yul, you must also understand something of our life here. My dictionary will not help you, in spite of its being my life's work. Dr Martin failed; not everyone can attain the truth of the high mountains.

But I digress once more.

When I first saw the children, I had renounced any hopes of man/woman love. Yet, barely thirty, I was not too old to feel maternal cravings. I loved Prilla and Yerom and for that I have suffered.

They arrived at that time of year when the gods are active and participate in our daily lives. Although our villages are Buddhist, Buddha has not squeezed out the local deities any more than he has rejected Our Lord. The gods co-exist on the brightly painted altars and each accepts the faithfuls' offerings. (How Dr Martin hated the gods' merriment. His god was exclusive, admitting no other colleagues. Typhus alone did not kill the good priest – he died broken-hearted.)

At the end of summer, after harvest, the gods from each mountain village are taken to visit one another. Everyone celebrates, as the red and gold effigies, almost concealed by the dancing throng, are dragged from village to village. It always reminds me of King David dancing before the ark of the Lord. Have you ever danced before the Lord, Mr Cox-Williamson? Of course not – a foolish question.

Now that year, on the final day of the festival, a tribe of gypsies descended with the swiftness of snow leopards through the high passes. Fortunately, they intended no harm, merely wishing to trade woollen goods and yak produce for corn and metal work. Without asking the elders' permission, they pitched their tents in the apricot orchards. What vagabonds they were, with long hair falling to their shoulders, their ears pierced with large silver rings, dressed in sheepskins turned inside out. They bristled with ammunition pouches. Their silky-haired terriers rode on the ponies' backs and snapped at our village dogs. Such tall and strikingly handsome people, who joked and laughed amongst themselves.

At noon, Joseph brought a basket of yak cheese from the strangers' camp: – Mem-sahiba, they wish to show you something.

A rich harvest of golden-globed apricots hung ready for plucking; I hoped they would not steal too many. I greeted their chief, an imposing woman bedizened with silver and turquoise jewellery. Her two husbands hovered nearby, slapping their thighs each time she made a joke. As the news of my arrival spread through the camp, more and more people crowded into the hairy, black tent to observe 'the long, yellow nose of the lama pilling.' Cups of chang were produced. The woman chief asked whether I was married and on learning that I was not, pushed one of her husbands towards me. At my blush, she guffawed.

- So you have no children?

- No, I have none.

In the heat and smoke, my head began to ache; I bent under the tent flap to go outside and relieve myself. The gypsies' ponies, tethered to the apricot trees, whickered. I had drunk too much *chang*. My head was fuddled; my hair came unpinned and fell about my shoulders. The sight of the village, the sound of the gypsies' merriment faded away. Some sort of vision, some sort of hallucination came to me. I don't know why: I am not an imaginative woman.

Through swirling tongues of mist, the fluid shapes of two children, boy and girl, solidified. Between them stood a man – Robbie. The boy held his left, the girl held his right hand. Robbie placed his palms flat against their backs and gently pushed them ahead into a field, bright with poppies. Instead of corn, the field grew crosses, thousands upon thousands of white wooden crosses. I have never seen Robbie's grave. The children hung back, looking at me. Those dream children had blue eyes, like his, like mine. Robbie smiled. They faded with him into the field of crosses.

I pinned up my hair and returned to the tent. The *chang* was circulating freely. Someone clasped my hand and pulled me into the fire circle. And there in front of me were two children! Real live ones! And their eyes, too, were blue, shining incongruously in grimy faces and around the boy's head, a white cloth sticky with blood. The girl clutched the boy's hand. Not unkindly, the chief prodded the girl's stomach.

- They're thin; they will not speak.

One of the chief's husbands, hunting wild goat, had found the children wandering half-starved, in a remote mountain pass. Before the visit was concluded, the chief had handed over the children and promised to return after winter to collect them. I never saw her or her sycophantic husbands again.

Possibly she believed the children feeble-minded. Possibly she believed them bewitched. Their resemblance to one another, those vivid blue eyes, proclaimed them brother and sister. I judged the girl about ten and her brother perhaps thirteen – their skin so grained with dirt that the first imperative was a bath. They followed me without a murmur; my heart was singing.

Joseph filled the tin tub that had almost cost the life of a mule to carry over the passes. The girl whimpered but when I untangled her long black hair and rubbed yak butter on her face to soften her cracked cheeks, she leant against my breast and that touch kindled such love, I almost wept. The boy refused my ministrations. Tsering bathed him, and then we dressed them in brown, woollen robes. They ate porridge and drank goat's milk with wary, delicate movements. Their lice-infested hair, I would deal with later.

I placed the children in the room next to mine and Joseph prepared beds from straw-filled mattresses, which I covered with bearskins. The girl, given my mirror, at first cried in surprised alarm, then flashed it around the room, reflecting the oil lamps, her brother's face and mine. I mimed that they must go to bed. They obeyed instantly. Ashamed to spy on them, I convinced myself that the end justified the means and listened, ear pressed behind the closed door. I heard the boy murmuring, although I couldn't distinguish in what language.

Laying aside my word lists for the dictionary, each morning I taught them and they learnt with an astonishing rapidity. Their names I discovered were Yerom and Prilla. Fearful of upsetting their equilibrium, I eschewed any questions; they volunteered no information. Our simple life, our simple food, suited them. Within months they were plump, smiling, healthy with rose-splashed cheeks on their copper-coloured skin. In spite of the icy winds and the short winter days, Yerom would often lean against the stone chorten built at the outskirts of the village, gazing north. Taller than the other lads, he soon became the fastest rider when the boys galloped our long-maned, wild-eyed ponies across the bouldered floor of a vanished glacier. Prilla was different. Knickknacks amused her, a thimble, a pair of scissors, an old game of Snakes and Ladders. Seldom did she stray from my side. Turning the pages of a tattered copy of *The Illustrated London News*, she pointed to a picture of an omnibus: – And what is that, Ama?

That first winter they spent amongst us piled up memories of a sweetness unparalleled in my experience (except for my brief months with Robbie). By the time that the apricot trees blossomed, I could no longer imagine life without them. Before the short monsoon, at the height of summer, Yerom left his post at the chorten and leant against my knee, while I sewed a blouse for Prilla. They were now speaking English with charming accents. They called me Ama. My love for them deepened, as their trust of me grew. They possessed a stillness unusual in such young children. Given time I felt sure, the mystery of their origin would be revealed. And it would be Prilla not Yerom. One day, the child, her tongue gripped between her teeth, drew a tall man and woman standing outside a round thatched hut. The roof shape different to anything in our area.

- What have you drawn?

She ran outside and would not answer.

How brief the time of happiness compared to the time of grief! That year I did not dread the twenty hours of winter dark now that our house, like every other in the village, resounded with children's laughter.

- That brilliant lad, said Dr Martin, must be sent away to school.
- They are happy here in the mission, I argued.
- Have you no thought for their future?

Of course I had. What better future could they have than to live surrounded with our love?

On cloudless winter nights the sky's black veil was pierced by the vivid rays of thousands of stars reflected like wavering torches in the waters of the Nag Chu, which flowed placidly through our fields. In houses warmed with dried yak dung, old men and women sung and chanted tales of gods and demons and peasants drank butter tea, cupful after cupful. Dr Martin thundered against idolatrous practices and raged whenever we took a flare in one hand and crept through the hard-packed snow to Lo Hensing's house to listen to the storytellers.

- We are only going to collect words for the dictionary, I told him. This partial truth stilled his complaints. Curiosity to learn more than words drew me. Coughing in the smoke-filled room, I drew the children within the circle of my arms.

The storytellers spoke of *kha-droma*, the sky-dancers, who are like our fairies, of the dong-dre, the demons, who steal the unwary soul, of hermits, who spend many years meditating in sealed-up caves. They spoke of magic and of corpses brought alive to dance. Between the discrete worlds of being and becoming hung the thinnest of veils. And sometimes, towards the end of a joyful evening, when the listeners grew reflective, the talk turned to Be-yul, the village which lies in a valley, unvisited for so long that it had become its own legend. The legend insisted that complete contentment exists in Be-yul, although why our peasants needed such a legend was inexplicable. Their lives were lapped with serenity: they ate what they grew; they wore what they spun. Neither the dictates of a distant government, nor the cajolings of a commerce as powerful as it was trivial, drove them. They had time to think and time to play. Poor in life's superfluities, they were rich in its essentials. As they worked they sang and what little they had, they shared. From the lofts above our heads descended the odours of a season's plenty, the smell of butter stored in tubs, the sweetness of dried apricots and the rancid smell of woollen fleeces.

A red-hat lama was visiting our lama. In a sonorous tone he spoke of lost legends and difficult magic. He had met a wandering yogin who claimed to have been to, and returned from, Be-yul.

- The way there is found through prayer and fasting. A fissure will appear in the glacier and you must jump. Your faith must be complete.

- It sounds like a sure death,' Our local language is difficult. I stressed the wrong syllable, informing the company that it sounded like a cracked teapot.

When the laughter had died down, Yerom, whose voice was rarely heard in any gathering, spoke: – If a river flows through Be-yul, there must be a way out and a way in. Did the yogin say?

The lama's eyebrows rose; children were not expected to question elders.

- Yerom, you know something of Be-yul? I whispered. What do you know? Where is it? To my questions, he remained silent.

In the mission, Dr Martin toyed with his watch chain. – Do you want to deprive these children, our holy charges, of the benefits of civilisation?

Prilla had accepted baptism; Yerom would not commit himself. So Reverend Martin worked on my conscience. His persistence wore down my resistance, until after the children's second winter with us, I agreed. Dr Martin arranged missionary scholarships in a church school in Surrey.

- We will write every week, Ama. Prilla's arm circled my waist. How keen she was to discover the rainbows spanning the country of her dreams. The word modern chimed in her ears like a silver bell. Of her brother's desires, I was uncertain. Everything I could teach him he had learnt and every book I possessed he had read. I fretted that such knowledge was gained at the expense of understanding. How could Yerom interpret Shakespeare? What could Dickens signify to one who had never seen a mean street nor performed a mean action? And towards the Bible, he developed a curious reluctance. – I don't admire a jealous God, he complained, nor one who seeks revenge. And of the New Testament, he simply said: – The disciples of Lord Jesus weren't as loyal as those of Lord Buddha. He showed as little desire to study with the lama as he did to learn Scripture with Dr Martin.

On our last evening, I tied their bundles together. Yerom sensed my unshed tears.

- It's necessary for me to go. I shall return, Ama. I have too much to remember. I shan't forget. And he gave me his rare smile.

Can I describe its brightness for you? I am no poet nor ever was. When the sun sets behind the mountains, the last ray lingers to caress the highest peak – that was Yerom's smile.

The children's' first letters read much as you would expect. Everything pleased Prilla: her school uniform, her classes, omnibuses, sausages for tea. Yerom's letters were more circumspect and I suspected that, accustomed like myself, to a rarefied air and a simplified life, the modern world's complexities presented him with ambiguities that bruised his spirit.

'... they speak many words, Ama but they do not act according to those same words. They say 'sorry' when they are not. 'Thanks' when they are not grateful. Neither space nor time exists in their lives. They stuff their houses with ugly objects. And often, they laugh and smile and shake their heads to one another but they aren't laughing inside, nor smiling with their eyes. The boys at my school push me against the wall. They call me yellow belly because I won't fight. They grow so angry when I will not answer them. I try to see far but I can't because chimneys block the horizon. The air smells of dirty smoke.'

I understood. After waving the children goodbye at the railhead in Darjeeling on their long journey to Bombay, I returned with relief to these mountains. Once I had crossed the final pass, I added a stone to the cairn on the summit, determined never to take that route again. And I never have!

At first their absence rubbed raw as an open wound. Gradually I became reconciled. My loneliness turned into solitude. I heard the silence of the mountains. As days, weeks and months piled into years, I learnt to reject the values that had brought me here; those waves of phenomenal appearances to which alone in our ignorance, we assign consistency and value. Yet in spite of this, I remained what I was, a missionary spinster.

Those years when the children lived amongst us are two pearls strung between the monotonous grey pebbles which represent the necklace of my life.

Shortly afterwards it seemed, although in calendar time it was several years later, the typhus epidemic killed both Martins. They are buried in the apricot orchard, so that each Spring, drifts of blossom smother their graves. I worked on the dictionary and found words to correspond to concepts that did not belong in our materialistic, practical world view: the transcendence of the soul, the nature of mind. Did my poor equivalents answer the purpose? For Be-yul, no English word expressed what I imagined its inner meaning. I could not attain enlightenment, cursed as I was with a doubting mind.

Like you, Mr Cox-Williamson, I am chained to the wheel of being, I can not avoid *samsara*. And gradually, in spite of my best intentions, my solitude grew irksome. Unlike the mountains, our purposes do not remain fixed. Our states of mind fluctuate. Those needs, those wants, those desires, I believed myself to have overcome, surfaced. I persuaded myself that the children, now grown, ought to return to help with the dictionary and with the faltering mission. Yerom and Prilla answered my letters separately.

Prilla's letter sparkled: she wrote of Neville, the youngest son of her foster family, who was taking her skating; of her foster mother – teaching her the use of a sewing machine; of herself, having cut and curled her hair (oh, Prilla, that lustrous black hair). 'So you may see, Ama, now is not the right time to return.'

Yerom had become his school's senior scholar: a note enclosed from the head-master mentioned a Cambridge scholarship, an outstanding talent for Mathematics, a most unusual boy, brilliant...

Was I to stifle their chances because I needed their company? Stay, stay, I encouraged.

Carved into a black boulder opposite the mission house was the sacred mantra *Om mani padme hum*. By murmuring it constantly, the sounds became as familiar as breathing. My attachments to the children slowly attenuated into shapes, insubstantial as the white cloud that wreathed Makula's peak. Once again, but at a high price, the loss of faith, I achieved peace.

Had the Martins lived, I might have remained a Christian. The empty stools on Sunday mornings mocked their efforts. (Joseph had returned to the fertile plains, overcome by the savage winters, and Tsering never converted.) Dr Martin prayed and Helga knelt. Their faith outweighed my own: while they lived, their certitudes enveloped me. But they did not live. Chance removed them. And the missionary society, 'with deep regret owing to financial constraints,' decided not to send any replacements. A decision neither unexpected nor unwise, since no converts demonstrated the superiority of our doctrine and only two children, one lame and the other feeble-witted, graced my schoolroom. The village sustained itself, as it had done for hundreds, nay thousands, of years, without benefit of Bible or sacraments. And I stayed.

Only Prilla, remained an ardent Christian: 'and Neville sings in the village choir... ' she wrote. Thus her request for permission to marry on her eighteenth birthday was not unexpected. Whatever my decision, my reply could not arrive until weeks after the date she had chosen. I granted permission nevertheless. A present? I could think of nothing from our seeming poverty which could add to her apparent riches.

Yerom's letters came less often – from monthly to quarterly then nothing for half-a- year. Of his sister's marriage, he wrote: 'Her spirit is tamed. She is happy in this place of here and now. In spite of her promise to our father, she has forgotten where she came from. I feel betrayed, Ama.' He had written 'our father.' Incomprehensible until I realised that Yerom referred to a time before I knew them. He wrote of 'our father'. Was he now ready to tell me? I would ask. My letter slipped into the saddlebag of Tsering's mule to start its perilous journey to the railhead. Months passed and no reply came. And I imagined that as his sister immersed herself in duties and pleasures of marriage, so he immersed himself in the circumscribed world of study.

My dictionary was complete – even the word for aeroplane – metal bird which flies. To occupy myself, I began a collection of folk tales and legends in which this region abounds. And the village lama, my friend, was eager to help. I wished, without quite knowing why, to learn more of Be-yul's mysteries.

- To reach the village the searcher must stand on the glacier's rim, close his eyes and jump. And if he maintains perfect faith, his eyes will open in Be-yul.

Yes, had I not heard that legend, years ago in Lo Hensing's house? Then as now, I was disappointed. Blind faith has never appealed. And once within, was there no way out, no way forward. A shut-in community. How claustrophobic! How did the inhabitants trade or marry, how... ?

The lama gave a loving smile; he was a saintly man. Did I wish to find the route myself? No, I had no intention. Ah, then, was not my interest misplaced.

- Leave Be-yul hidden in its mists. It will be better so.

In plain words he was telling me to mind my own business.

*

Prilla married. Prilla moved to Bermondsey with her Neville. 'Imagine, we go to the pictures every Saturday night. The cinema organ plays. There are always such crowds around us. Only sometimes,' she wrote, 'I remember the sound of silence.'

I understood that the world was changing. I understood that Prilla, with the same enthusiasm that she played with my music box, had adapted to the life that Neville offered. In the photo she sent, her bobbed hair lay against her cheeks in corrugated waves. Her lips were darkened. Her sailor-suited son sat high in a perambulator. Had she returned here, I should have no perambulator to offer, no hairdresser. My dear little Prilla.

Yerom remained in Cambridge and accepted a fellowship. He wished that I could be present at his graduation ceremony. 'Since my real mother cannot... ,' he wrote. This was the second mention of any time before he lived with us in Dzam Po. Ah, I had not wished to name our village. It does not signify. How foolish to try to hide. Did not your letter find me! How can anything remain hidden now that aeroplanes criss-cross every valley and strip away the highest peaks' mysteries, reducing them to a postcard on sale in a crowded bazaar?

And then the longed-for letter arrived from Yerom:

'Life glitters like the tinsel on the Christmas tree which the college sets up in the Common Room. That tree is fake – only an amputated stump. I, too, am rootless. I can find no role. Only my professor inspires me. With his failing eyes, through icicle-thick glasses, he peers at a world of number. He is like the red hat lama, do you remember? My mathematical studies draw me into a world of clarity. I am almost convinced at these times that the solutions I seek lie in the world of science. It envelops the professor like the clouds above Makula. At last I find silence. Yet, whenever I find it, I hear the gongs. They will not leave me. They sound louder and louder. They summon me to a place existing somewhere beyond the professor's certitudes. Am I still pure enough? Will my father be happy to learn what he has missed and what he has been spared? Prilla believes that Be-yul was only a childish game that we invented between ourselves. I wish that I could believe her. Her memories are short-lived, brittle as the life she leads. If Be-yul exists, my task is to find it.'

I was going to see him again!

The letter ended: 'And we shall meet shortly. We have received permission. The expedition has received funds from the Royal Geographic Society.'

The whole village streamed down the mountain side, dogs barking, children beating drums, to welcome Yerom and the four young men he brought with him. The excitement caught us all.

- I am so happy to see you. I had almost lost hope, Yerom. He must have been about twenty-four years old.

- You lack faith, Ama,' said Yerom. His smile was unchanged; my heart sang.

On their first night, I found the young men's size, their vigour overwhelming. Their porters pitched tents in the same orchard where the warrior gypsies had camped ten years earlier. So many porters – twenty men for four Europeans. Was Yerom an European? His features were decidedly Asiatic but no one had ever seen an Asiatic with eyes of translucent blue. To be an European meant something in those days. Does anyone still find it important? I do not.

That evening, leaving his friends in their tents, he stood beside me as he used to do, one hand on my left shoulder. His companions' merry shouts disturbed the evening calm. I believe they were playing cards: something I have never been able to abide.

- They are capital fellows. Yerom smiled – a caution residing in his gaze that had not been there before.

Why was he conducting this expedition when he was a mathematician with a brilliant career waiting and the season too far advanced to explore unmapped terrain? The first flurries of snow had already covered the fields. Leaves spun like gold coins on the poplars lining the village. The shepherds had brought their flocks down from the high pastures; the harvest was already threshed and stored.

- You're walking off the map, Yerom.

- I can always walk back on, Ama.

- Why must you do this?

White triangles of prayer flags fluttered from the chorten; an eagle aloft on a thermal current, hung motionless dark wings against a darkening azure sky. Peak upon peak stretched away northwards, floating in a coral sunset. The detachment I had practised during the years of his absence faltered; tears wetted my cheeks.

- I can find the way back, Yerom insisted.

- How? Tell me, tell me more. I know so little.

- Ama, do you truly wish it?

- Truly.

Bringing two bearskins out of the house, he draped them across our shoulders. Butter lamps winked from darkened houses; smoke curled from twenty roofs. Layer upon layer, screen upon screen, the stars appeared, dotting the sky with question marks.

- Your eyes are blue. Why?

- My father had blue eyes inherited from his father and his father's father. His voice was so low, so unhappy, that I almost gestured him to stop. Our civilisation's curse, as the old lama knew, is our passion for facts. Mystery appals us. I did not stop Yerom. Indeed, I urged him to continue.

- The Europeans sent many expeditions into the mountains wanting to find so many different things, did they not?

I nodded: the valley dwellers believe that men are not meant to trespass in the abode of the Gods. Now that nearly every mountain has been climbed and nearly every route mapped, the grand adventure is almost complete. Where have the gods gone? Should not some snows have been left untrampled, some mysteries left unsolved?

- Am I not right to go?

I had no answer.

- You remember listening outside our door when we first came?

- Forgive me. I didn't mean to...

- It doesn't matter any longer. I wanted to tell you even then but I'd promised my father silence until...

- Until what?

Yerom sighed:

- Until I was strong enough to return and find them. My father told me what he imagined outside Be-yul. His stories were confused, his words bitter. Was the world beyond our precipices a heaven or a hell? Why must our lives be spent in a cloud of unknowing? My father stood in front of the hut, hour upon hour, scanning the blocked pass, the tumbled rocks. My mother grew unhappy with his restlessness. They quarrelled bitterly when they thought we couldn't hear them.

Then I realised something of which I'd for long been semi-consciously aware; that Yerom and Prilla's spoke a mountain peoples' dialect mingled with English words. I was bewildered and frightened.

- I can't grasp this, Yerom.

He put an arm around my shoulders. Spoke lightly of his friends, of college, of insignificant events. And beneath the seeming nonchalance of our words lay his unspoken desire to find a place that maybe did or did not exist.

What he had not told me he left for me to read. An old journal lay on my bed, pages creased and yellow; the date 1862. He had used my spectacle case as a paperweight. I read the underlined passage:

UNSOLVED MYSTERIES OF OUR TIME

The Royal Society financed the expedition of Captain Jerome Youngland, which was undertaken in the High Himalayas on the

Tibetan Chinese border. The declared purpose of the expedition was to ascertain the geographical location of a valley called Be-Yul. Captain Youngland, accompanied by his wife Priscilla, set out in February 26th 1856. The inclusion of a lady in the expedition was considered ill-judged. After his preliminary reports from Dzam Pho in April, 1856, no more were received. The members of the expedition vanished as completely as if they had been led astray by the Pied Piper. A search party which left from Darjeeling in the following Spring found no trace. Rumours have persisted that Captain Youngland had made an amazing discovery...

I read no further. In spite of what your letter leaves unwritten, I have guessed the object of your search, Mr David Cox-Williamson. Your letterhead gives the clue: Director – Consolidated Mining. What might those two Victorian explorers have discovered? Deep beneath the rocks, gold and uranium lie buried. Our people do not want it brought to the surface. The earth they say is our mother and must not be wounded. Do not mount the third expedition to find Be-yul, I implore you.

*

My foster son and his companions set forth without their porters, who, at that time of year, refused to go further for any amount of wages.

- Our equipment is the most modern available, the young men boasted.

They carried tinned foods, sleeping bags of goose feathers, stoves to melt their drinking water, tents to withstand blizzards.

- We'll reach the valley before winter sets in, they insisted.

- You will have to stay until the passes reopen.

Yerom's smile had lost none of its compelling brilliance.

- Come with us, Ama?

Why not indeed! What kept me attached to my daily world. Work? No. Friends? No. Family? All were dead. Only one tie remained – Prilla.

- She'll never return, said Yerom, they've taught her the fear of silence and the dislike of solitude.

- Aren't you chaps ready? cried the tallest young explorers, who wore a tweed cap rakishly over one eye.

- No, I shall stay here, I told my foster son, and wait.

Later that winter, this cap was found only three miles away, frozen solid in a glacier. Next Spring, a yak caravan bringing wool and salt through the high passes, observed the vulture-eaten remains of two men and six ponies in the bottom of a ravine. Purple primulas bloomed in the crevasses of the rocks; the snow melted.

Yerom never returned.

After three further years, I decided to travel to England. I do not know why in my solitude I indulged so far-fetched a hope that Prilla would rejoin me? My preparations began. Tsering, with great glee, had bartered a two month old copy of *The Times* from the gypsies for a cup of salt. The date was September 3rd, 1939. I postponed my departure. Cowardice? Fear?

In 1942, I received a next-of-kin letter: a rocket bomb had wiped out Prilla, her baby boy and Neville, who had been with them on a weekend leave. I put her photograph in the locket I always wear, opposite Robbie's. Now both photographs are unrecognisable. You would expect a photograph to fade in almost fifty years.

*

I have now waited for almost a lifetime, sitting in this high-backed chair which faces the mountain peaks. I expect Yerom. How do I know that he lives? You will find this hard to believe, Mr Cox-Williamson but I have seen his face reflected in the waters of lake Mansovar. It is a holy lake and the waters cannot lie. The surface of the water rippled, disturbed by a flock of snow geese rising. Thus I could not tell whether the face was smiling. Yet I believe that Yerom will find a way out of Be-yul. There must be one. Perhaps a dive into the river which will rush underground and emerge with the swimmer half-drowned on the other side of the gorge? Such things are known in these regions. Did not the yogin return?

You see I do not believe that Jerome and Priscilla Youngland perished on their expedition. I believe that hand in hand they leapt in perfect faith towards a future they imagined led to perfect contentment. Thus they completed their lives in the valley beyond the furthest peaks. I can almost hear your laughter, David Cox-Williamson.

- That crazy old biddy's stuck up on a mountain alone so long.

Are you waiting for the happy ending? There is one – of a sort. My necessity has become my virtue. The villagers revere me for a holy woman. In the mornings small gifts lie on my doorstep: a bowl of yoghurt, a basket of eggs, an embroidered hat. These gifts are unwanted but I cannot prevent them. I have waited and continue to do so. In Be-yul, Jerome and Priscilla Youngland, escaping the trammels of Victorian convention, were happy, I know. I believe it. I, who have never, since my girlhood, known a kiss of passion, imagine theirs. The bullet that smashed Robbie's life ended that part of mine. Not so for them. They found Be-yul, and they did not want it to change. And I imagine how they persuaded the inhabitants, delighted with their strange blue eyes, impressed with their confidence and skills, to seal the pass, to seal the pass and forget the way out. To live that life, to choose that simplicity, was no hardship for them. She would have learnt to spin; he, to master the simple techniques of husbandry and metalwork. Can you not see them playing – creating a real life dolls' house, a simple life enriched with what they had brought from an inventive, enterprising world? And little by little, in the dance of time, they discarded their habits and prejudices. How do I know this? Because I have done something similar myself. Only in my case, I have largely been alone and they had one another. Coming from an ants termite, they identified with the snow goose, who mates for life and soars across the sky. And deliberately they pinioned their own wings, turning their backs upon your reality, Mr Cox-Williamson, because it was harsh; because they did not wish to wear cloth spun in mills worked by children; nor eat animals slaughtered in abattoirs. They chose and chose freely. In the privacy of their minds, they kept what they needed from the world of Wordsworth and Shakespeare and Milton and let the rest evaporate. Their solution must have seemed to them perfection. They sought and they found – silence. The happy ending!

But the ending after the ending – don't imagine that it will be happy. It won't. That has always been the problem with perfection: it remains so fleeting in the eye of God. Not so for their descendants. Not enough enchantment remained to appease the generations of blue-eyed sons that followed, inheriting a shut-in kingdom from their blue-eyed fathers. If there was no stress, no strife, no competition in that hidden valley; there was neither freedom, nor choice. With only good offered, they could not refuse evil. The rule was benevolence itself but it was not free. Why else should Yerom's bitter father have pushed him and his little sister into the underground passage – space enough for a child where a man was too bulky to wriggle through? What other explanation is there? How else could he have risked their lives, had he not believed they were finding freedom?

Yerom carried six sticks of dynamite in his pack. He will decide whether to use them and blast a way out. He has a choice. Will he bring his people back with him? Maybe he will decide that the way out entails more suffering than to stay where he is. He has stayed there now for many years. The father he sought must be long dead. Has he taken his place? My blue-eyed foster son is now nearly as old as I was when he left. It is more than fifty years since we waved goodbye.

Tomorrow, Tsering's grandson will take these papers. In some months they will find your desk, Mr Cox-Williamson. What sense will you make of them?

*

My name is Heather Dodrington. I came to Dzam Po in 1925. I am still waiting. And I shall wait until...

-oOo-

Lottie's
Little
Habit

Charlotte admired the Lycra 40 denier clinging to slender ankles. Nice thing about legs – they keep their shape. Pity you can't say the same about faces. Good bone structure in place but gravity, pinching tiny, vertical lines above her upper lip, whispered, 'You'll be a fifty-something soon.' The mirror, though, was ever so pretty and had been one of her finest, spontaneous coups.

It had beckoned in the basement of The Canvaserai, a shop catering for well-heeled New Agers, where a dun-coloured assistant appearing in the incense-laden gloom – offered, 'to pop down to the stock room and see whether we've a larger one in stock.' Charlotte, who'd had the foresight to equip herself with a gold-lettered Canvaserai plastic bag, slipped the mirror inside and sauntered towards the exit, examining healing crystals en route.

At this point she'd been having 'goes' for three months, growing bolder with each expedition. Of all the objects crammed into the sitting room, ranging from the practical (electric can opener) to the vulgar (plastic Taj Mahal) her favourites were the china dogs. She would've kept a dog if her lease had allowed. A fluffy pup – wouldn't it be nice? Gregory had insisted she rent a maisonette in a good neighbourhood. But the conversion was tacky, cheap. Bonny and her sister never chose to stay, preferring their father's split-level in Highgate and his new lady – the winsome Evelyn. So unfriendly the girls, as if they blamed her !

Middle-aged man running off with secretary – what a cliché! I need something to cuddle, murmured Charlotte.

She was sentimental. Bred by Nature for cosy, well-beloved motherhood, genetics had dealt an unfair hand, giving her appearance of dark-haired, chiselled beauty with improbably long legs that was wildly at odds with her innermost self. With those looks – a model, or an actress, or a dancer: that's what Poppa said she had to be. Her portfolio of photographs was stunning, her speaking voice mellifluous, her smile dazzling. Yet she never landed anything but minor roles. Poppa put it down to luck: lack of-. But Charlotte knew better; her acting was lousy, although she possessed deft fingers (so useful for her present activities). Good thing Poppa wasn't alive to see. She hadn't intended... the habit, the hobby, call it what you will, had infiltrated her life so insidiously that at first she'd hardly realised. She'd been sitting in the flat's only armchair, trying to convince herself she enjoyed the view of municipal park beds tulip-ed as far as the eye could see, wondering vaguely whether she was angry and if so – with whom? Six months into Gregory's departure with Evelyn; seven weeks since she'd heard from either of the girls; a week since she'd met a friend; three days since she'd chatted to an acquaintance and twenty-four hours since she'd spoken to a living soul. The headiest excitement of the coming week would be changing her library books, What activity remained except shopping!

Aimlessly, she trundled a lop-sided, spiteful trolley around Sainsburys and ripped open the Cadbury's Flake selected for watching East Enders and absentmindedly chewed. Muzak was playing. The checkout girl waved her articles across the scanner, tut-tutting until it pinged and never glanced into the bottom of the trolley. The moment to butt in, 'You've left this out,' evaporated. Lottie paid her £22.74 and pushed the guilty trolley at a run into the car park.

'Don't you dare ever do that again, wicked girl,' Grandma Merschner slaps and hisses, THOU SHALT NOT STEAL, as a tiny hand reaches out for the sweets displayed so temptingly at six-year old eye level. Forty-two years later, Charlotte Green (née Merschner) flinches from the memory of that undeserved slap. But this time she's got away with it. Easy. Like losing your virginity. Once you've done it – you wonder what the fuss was about?

A tasty habit develops on her weekly Sainsbury trips: a bit of chocolate here; a few grapes there, a nibble of pistachio nuts. What choice! Boxes of kiwis, kumquats, grapes, passion fruit. Pop a selection into the outsize coat pocket – only one piece of each. Don't be greedy. Be swift. Charlotte procrastinates, her fingers hovering between Cape gooseberry and mango. A moon-faced child, squinting at her from beneath the brim of a floppy, floral hat, whines, 'Mum-ee, gimme strawberry like that lady did put in her pocket.' Charlotte cringes at the whoosh of a slap. 'Shut your mouth, Sharon and stop bothering folk.'

After these lunches, thanks to Tescos, Sainsburys and Safeways she cuts out supper on shopping days and housekeeping bills show a welcome diminution. She tells herself every day: I am going to stop this silly habit but she doesn't.

Her agent phones: 'Do keep in touch, Sweetie. Might have a voice-over next month.' Discouraged, she walks into Marks & Spencer.

SHOPLIFTERS WILL BE PROSECUTED. How unfriendly! Greg used to complain: 'You never rise to challenges.' He should see her now! Charlotte, using her Glasgow accent, trills: 'Och, I'm sae sorry, lassie, nothing fits,' and strolls out with a pink cotton blouse under her sweater and a most useful pair of candy-striped leggings under her jeans.

A hobby – that's all it is... a hobby – nothing more... I can stop whenever I choose. And she even looks better, younger, with almost daily doses of excitement.

In the window at Circe's sale, she sees: £150 shoes reduced £50 ONLY – way outside her budget. A trick of mind-boggling simplicity. 'Can I try these on – the pair, please?' A quick walk up and down the showroom, edging towards open plate glass doors, the assistant vanishing to bring shoes for another customer; nip outside, leave scuffed-toe black flatties discarded beside the assistant's stool and Charlotte has slipped in among Saturday shoppers. THOU SHALT NOT STEAL booms a metallic voice. She freezes: it's only the town clock striking five.

Moses had omitted an eleventh commandment – THOU SHALT BE PRUDENT. Boots had a revolving black globe with eight winking red eyes. Charlotte believed it a sham. It wasn't. The case before the Colchester Magistrates Court came up one month later undefended. Plea – Guilty. Fine – one hundred pounds. She cowered at home, wishing she had a pet to cuddle or a friend to commiserate. Daren't tell Gregory or the girls. Waited for the commotion to blow over. No such luck! She had made a dreadful mistake and written 'actress' instead of 'housewife' on the charge sheet. A paragraph in the local newspaper read: Charlotte Green, actress, pleaded guilty to stealing a hairbrush worth 85d... The story should have slipped from everyone's consciousness. And would have, had not a London freelance, appropriately named Amanda Fox-Gibbon, spent her Mondays sifting local rags for possible angles. The word 'actress' caught the ambitious, young fox's eye. A little predatory digging and the bare bones of Charlotte's nugatory career were exhumed. Some barer than others. In early days Charlotte Merschner had posed for a camera club. Amanda tracked down Charlotte, whose touching interview brought out all of Amanda's sympathies. She wrote: 'HUBBY'S NEGLECT MADE EX-ACTRESS STEAL'.

August is silly season for newspapers. Terrorists lie low and politicians head for the sun. The other SUN picked up on the story and dug out another pic – this one full-frontal – with the caption WHERE DID LOTTIE PUT HER BRUSH? across the embarrassing bit. That should have been the end of a silly nine-days wonder.

Only it wasn't.

What happens when you are in the right place at the right time? Publicity – that's what. Liza Farhquarson was doing one of her late night TV specials: *The Menopause – Cause or Effect?* She had an amazing line up: Germaine Greer for the oldies, Helena Kennedy for the legal angle, the blonde lady rabbi, Julia Neuberger, Susie Orbach to give the therapeutic angle and some promise of Camille Paglia flying over for the penile one. Liza visited Lottie and was shown china dogs, lamp shades, sweaters, scarves, books, face-creams, trinkets, shoes and given the story behind each. Liza entertained highly articulated notions of womens' oppression and patriarchal property rights; 'You'll fit in very well, dear. Just be yourself.' The programme clocked up a gratifying score in the ratings.

Amanda Fox-Gibbon paid Lottie another visit. They went walkabout down Colchester High Street. Amanda wrote the story up in *The Observer* and spared no details, including her thighs sticky with excitement, when the manager walked past them and both women had buckled on Italian leather belts at £22 each. Amanda of course later paid in full, explained it was for a story and settled the matter.

Libby Purves invited Charlotte onto MIDWEEK along with a feminist writer, a liberal bishop, an industrial psychologist and a supermarket manager, on the theme: *Society Creates Criminals*. She was the star of the show. Especially when she remarked in her clear, little-girl voice with its delicate hint of sadness: 'And everything I'm wearing – including my underwear, I have to tell you comes from one of my 'goes'.

The bishop's horrified cry of 'What! Stolen knickers!' made every paper.

Letters of support came pouring in. Charlotte found herself popular, sought after, invited to give interviews, appear on Chat Shows. One question that no one could quite bring themselves to ask (she appeared so fragile) was whether she was still indulging?

By the time parliament resumed, she remained hot news. With Amanda's help, she wrote a clutch of articles for the broadsheets. Her photo was in *Marie-Claire* and *Cosmopolitan*. Unfortunately for national morality, Charlotte proved neither capable of lying nor interested in holding anything back. She detailed every little trick and subterfuge. They proved extraordinarily easy to copy: chatting up the check-out girl so she doesn't notice the dozen beer cans on the bottom of the trolley; holding brand-new gloves in your left hand; keeping on the new bra and slipping your old one in to the box; eating a sandwich and losing the wrapping. Some 'goes' were breathtakingly simple (possibly an acting background helped) like putting on a matching coat and hat and walking out of the store. She managed a similar trick at the Garden Centre with a five foot bay tree tucked under her arm but having no garden, left it in front of the Cat Rescue.

A rash of copycat 'goers' copied her tips. If her story had evoked public sympathy, her activities uncovered a public need. Her exploits validated thousands of middle-aged women, who found getting older had taken the zing out of their lives. Whether or not they had enough money, it did not seem enough. The buzz was missing; the shops were tempting. The growing legion of 'goers' found in Charlotte Green (née Merschner) an exciting role model. Even such an apparently put-together journalist as Amanda Fox-Gibbon enjoyed a little flutter; a lottery in which you were guaranteed a prize, provided that you kept a cool head. The ongoing wave swept the country from Harrogate to Brighton, from Edinburgh to Plymouth, not sparing the wife of 'Disgruntled, Tunbridge Wells'. Store-managers suffered audibly.

Sunday columnists devoted enthusiastic inches to this new sociological phenomenon. A Southern Counties Tory asked plaintively during Prime Minister's Question Time: 'Is every middle-aged woman in Great Britain shoplifting?' The Prime Minister, who had half an hour earlier been informed of an unexplained absence of lavatory rolls and soap in the Ladies, ashtrays and teaspoons in the Members Dining room, replied that, 'Figures are notoriously difficult to come by.' A Royal Commission was set-up, upon which various distinguished ladies declined to sit. French correspondents sent ecstatic copy home describing *la nouvelle maladie Anglaise*.

Charlotte, bemused by fame, installed an answerphone.

The answerphone was a Godsend; she prayed that it wouldn't break down. Naturally she had no Guarantee and had suffered a few qualms over that phone – at £120 rather dearer than her usual prizes. The bespectacled, spotty Dixon's assistant had aroused her maternal instinct but she'd been unable to resist the temptation. Nowadays her notoriety made such exploits impossible.

Messages received: from Bonny – 'am enthralled' – from Gillian – 'am simply appalled' from Greg – 'am appealing to what family feeling you have left. How on earth can I continue as a Tax Inspector?'

A new Charlotte was emerging. At last her personality matched her looks. An offer arrived from her agent, two offers in fact, a part in a TV sitcom and some modelling. She said: 'Later perhaps, I need time to look around.'

On returning home from London by train – no 'goes'; nothing more exciting than a magazine in which she found two references to herself – she listened to a message from a Miz Claire Din in Bradford. The voice was honey-brown, Yorkshire and insistent. Charlotte poured herself a gin and dialled.

Claire Din, a midwife originally from Tobago, had founded *The Clandestine Club*. To join you had to give (a) proof of being female, either biologically or psychologically, and (b) hand in an entrance fee of £150 worth of nicked stuff. The club had a waiting list. There was talk of setting up branches. Would Charlotte come and address the first AGM? In private of course.

Charlotte would.

Claire said, smiling: 'I thought you'd be older.'

Lottie said, smiling: 'I thought you'd be younger.'

The AGM was a rib-clutching success, as member after member recounted exploits of astounding ingenuity. One frail old lady had taken to dining in restaurants with a handful of dead flies in a polythene bag in her pocket. She'd eat three-quarters of a nourishing plateful, insert her useful fly and call for the manager. The only drawback was that she was running out of restaurants.

After the meeting finished with 'Three cheers for Lottie,' Charlotte and Claire stayed up the whole night talking; they had two lifetimes to compare.

The organisation was forced underground – too many prosecutions. Charlotte moved up to Bradford to advise.

And the rest is history.

Claire has given up midwifery. The two women run SA (Shoplifters Anonymous) their country-wide workshops which are so tremendously popular that there's a scheme afloat to export them to California. The rumour (unproved) is circulating that the workshops are a fraud – nothing more than a front. Shoplifting isn't cured by becoming anonymous.

Gillian changed her surname. Gregory lost his job; Evelyn found a younger bloke. Charlotte has two hundred and fifty china dogs.

Charlotte shares Claire's flat. They're keen on Yoga. Their SA activities keep them fully occupied. They are daffily in love and numbers of middle-aged women are brighter-eyed than they used to be. The fall in supermarket profits has continued.

-oOo-

The
Matriarch

lways tell lies, Rachel,' Grandma used to say. 'Always tell lies. A
woman's job is to keep the peace.'

In spite of that, I always hoped that her version of her own story
was true. Born eldest child and only daughter of Romanian Jews,
fleeing one pogrom or another, which one was never told us, she was
born and grew up in Whitechapel, where her parents kept a dairy. At
twelve, she learned to play the piano; at eighteen she fell in love with
a violinist. Her parents forbade the marriage. They encouraged (she'd
never admit forced) her into accepting the courtship of Abraham
Levine, a small-sized, small-time businessman. The telling always ended
with a triumphant: 'Never married, never, my violinist. Died fifty years
later – a bachelor.'

That was another of her lessons; true love is never consummated
and never dies.

And love, for my grandma, had nothing to do with sex. Thirteen
children were born over twenty-three years. 'And never once saw me
naked, never.'

'So how'd you do it, Grandma?'

'In the dark, of course. He lifted my nightie.'

Out of those thirteen babies, only eight survived long enough to
grow up. Scary tales were told of flu epidemics, of diphtheria, of
charwomen substituting bleach for barley water in baby's bottle. Not a
single one was breastfed.

'Never had enough milk.' With pleased delicacy, she patted her black crepe bodice and added darkly: 'Blood is thicker than water.'

And she taught other lessons, bewilderingly contradictory in their message. Girl babies were inferior to boy babies, daughters came second to sons but women were always, in every respect, superior to men, 'the dirty beasts!'

Shortly after baby Cyril's curls were cut, Abie Levine succumbed to a heart attack. Had he indulged in too much nightie-lifting? Grandma never accused him openly of being, one of the dirty beasts. You were expected to draw your own conclusions. For the rest of her life, she wore black crepe, enlivened with crocheted lace collars, except on special occasions like weddings or barmitsvahs when her grey silk made an appearance.

Once during her long widowhood, a eligible bachelor of seventy-two, invited her to the cinema.

'How was it, Grandma?'

'The dirty beast!' His hand had brushed against her arm during the performance.

Thereafter she'd only visit the pictures with grandchildren. We'd quiver with embarrassment as she'd call out to the heroine, 'Watch out! he's coming up behind you.'

In her seventies, she developed a fascination with sex. That sort of thing had never been discussed when her two daughters were growing up, except that both received a thorough grounding in its horrors. As a result, I suppose, the elder, Ginni, emigrated to America and no one would ever say what she did for a living; the younger, my mother, would never discuss anything that occurred below the waist.

But now Grandma asked questions of startling intimacy. Did I or my mates make love before marriage? How did we stop babies coming? Early old age had unbuckled the blinkers of that Victorian upbringing, sending her on a journey of discovery. Whether she ever regretted having set out fifty years too late, I never found out. The violinist was often mentioned during these sessions.

She lived in a ghetto built with walls stronger than brick and cement. Never admitting to fear or dislike of *goyim*, she said that they smelt peculiar. And since you could never marry one, why bother with social intercourse when sexual intercourse put you beyond the pale? When the district was colonised by Schwarzers, Pakistanis and West Indians – it wasn't their colour she objected to. As long as you were a Jew you could be as Chinese or Indian as you pleased.

Hers was a blessed and fortunate old age. She owned her semi-detached, sharing it with a married son, an unmarried son and aunt Ginni, who, from time to time, visited from her not-to-be-named occupations. Other sons and daughters lived locally except for Moishe, the black sheep. He went *mesuggah*, said Grandma.

At number twenty-seven the household bickered non-stop. Grandma the still centre of their turbulence; the eye of the hurricane when a real storm blew up.

She owned a slave – truly she did. Whatever the United Nations definition of slavery may be, any human being, totally dependant upon another's whims, working wageless, a seven-day week, must come pretty close. Hannah, a dumpy, pear-shaped woman with a sweet, childish voice, was married to uncle Nahum. After one still-born son, Hannah remained barren. 'A curse,' said Grandma. Auntie Hannele's life consisted of shopping, cooking, cleaning, washing, ironing, gardening, sewing and running errands for Mama and the rest of them. Auntie Ginni gave her cast-off, costume jewellery, my Mum cast-off clothes. Both her husband Nahum and her unmarried brother-in-law Cyril, bullied her.

'*Nebbich*, my poor Cyril,' Grandma would lament, 'never finds one good enough.'

And I believed every word.

Whenever Cyril brought home a Miriam or a Rachel, (nice girls every one, although 'girls' became increasingly euphemistic as Cyril's paunch increased) Grandma always spotted some flaw; some subtle reason why she wouldn't do. In any case, none could stand comparison with Mama. Early photos showed a black-haired, dark-eyed beauty. In old age she stooped, only size nine shoes remained as evidence of a once imposing height. Grandma's tone never varied; she never complained and never, never argued. An appropriate cliché smoothed over every situation. When Evie, one of her granddaughters, ran off with a commercial salesman and left inoffensive Arnold literally holding the baby, Grandma'd say: 'Never mind, Arnold, as good fish in the sea as ever came out.' When my own father suffered a minor heart attack she told my mother; 'No use crying over spilt milk. Len's got a good man, hasn't he?' When Hannah attempted a rare revolt, like tending a headache instead of frying fish, Grandma would say: 'A difficult girl but least said soonest mended and Hannele wouldn't leave me if someone offered her Buckingham Palace. I'll do anything for a quiet life.'

Hannah smothered by the feather bolster of Grandma's tolerance could only yield. And for the rest? The subterranean currents of family tensions ran through the sewers of our unconscious; no one dared lift the manhole covers.

In Grandma's house, you felt secure; bad things weren't allowed. In a war which nearly wiped out European Jewry – all that happened to our family – my Dad got piles in the ARP and a distant cousin developed Multiple Sclerosis. Grandma sent Cousin Laurie chicken soup, which took Aunt Hannah an hour each way on the bus to deliver but Grandma insisted. Aunt Hannah never dared admit that chicken soup gave Cousin Laurie heartburn.

After the war, on Sunday mornings, my cousins and I used to play in her narrow garden, in a shed crammed with objects that, 'might come in handy someday.' We'd spend hours crawling through tunnels of furniture, boxes, trunks, parcels of old newspapers.

One summer's day, I found a silver web hanging between lilac branches. A spider waited at one corner; an insect was trapped at the other, a soft, grey-bodied insect, its mouth opening and shutting in a scream too high for our ears. I almost worked up enough courage to tear down the web and let the insect escape. But Grandma taught us to be afraid of creepy-crawlies. And this was such a strange, ugly one. When we finished playing explorers and came blinking into the sunshine, the insect's body had been eaten. But the spider had stopped at the head, leaving the beaky mouth opening and shutting in that soundless scream. The web was still there, weeks later, binding the minute, intricate skeleton. In that cosy, private world that Grandma spun around her family – each of us so special – that incident remained the only bad memory I've kept from number twenty-seven.

Even so, once I'd grown up, we'd gone out together for a year before I felt brave enough to take Clive to Golders Green.

Hannele brought us into the front room, which smelt as usual of fried onions, Grandma's cologne and dust. A gas fire, burning full-blast, used up any spare oxygen. Brown velvet curtains were already drawn and a one-bar electric fire waited ready in Cyril's corner.

'He can't stand draughts,' said Aunt Hannah.

Every surface was spread with lace doilies, crocheted by Grandma herself, each covered with family photographs. Tacked to the flocked wallpaper, pictures of Crawfie and Lilibet, torn from *Woman's Own*, faced framed postcards of Ben Gurion and Chaim Weizmann.

'Don't do anything special for us, please, Grandma.'

'Who me? As if I would.'

Clive was told to sit in a leather armchair in front of the gas fire
'What's the matter, Clive? Tea not right?'
'No, no. A trifle warm, isn't it?'
'Keep your coat on a while. It's cold out.'
'But Grandma, it's stifling in here.'
'As you please, Charlotte. I hope the young man won't catch a chill. She's obstinate. Have you noticed yet, Clive?'
Without offending one of us, Clive couldn't reply, so went on eating the bread and jam, scones and biscuits heaped on his plate.

Meanwhile, Hannah had been preparing supper for the 'boys' aged at that time, fifty and thirty-five, respectively. They ate separately. My uncle Nahum arrived first, wearing overcoat, hat and muffler. Sitting with his back to us, he ate fried fish and chips, bread and butter, tinned peaches and custard. Hannah laid a dog-eared pile of *Tit-Bits* and *Reveilles* in front of his plate. She confided to Clive: 'So exhausted he is from his work. His brain needs a rest.' Throughout this meal, she stood behind his chair, scurrying out to the kitchen for more pickle or fresh tea.

Nahum addressed a single remark to Clive. 'Can't drink the muck they've given you, young man. Need a special brew. Delicate stomach, you know'. With a grunt, a belch and a fart, he picked up his funnies and departed for the back room.

Then Cyril arrived. Both returned from work at six o'clock but each preferring Grandma and Hannah's undivided attention, took turns to eat first.

'Kept a nice bit of boiled for you,' said Grandma, adding to Clive, 'He can't take fried. Delicate digestion – like mine.'

Hannah whined that boiled should've been kept for Nahum's delicate digestion and retreated complaining into the back room. Her husband's answering roar shook the partition wall. 'Silly cow. You know boiled lies on my guts.'

Aunt Ginni was staying that month, on one of her rare visits from New York. She lolled at the dining table, wearing purple and yellow flowered crêpe de chine, showing glimpses of lace-edged slip and blue-shadowed armpits. Considering herself on holiday, Aunt Ginni, waited on by Hannah, ate two plates of fried egg and würst and complained that the tea wasn't freshly made. 'Hannah,' she added, 'what're you thinking of? This young couple've had no supper.'

'That's true,' agreed Cyril, picking his teeth with a split matchstick and reading *The Jewish Chronicle*.

Grandma ignored my protests and a three course meal appeared. Chicken soup ('you won't get soup like this out of a tin') latkes, meatballs and strudel.

Clive ate with dogged politeness.

'Nice to see a young man with a proper appetite,' said Grandma, heaping Clive's plate. 'My boys won't eat a thing.'

Walking up the Golders Green Road towards the tube, Clive asked: 'Is it always like that?'

'No, not exactly. Everyone was on their best behaviour.'

'No one said a word!'

'Exactly. If you'd not been there, they'd have been rowing non-stop.'

'Gosh!' said Clive. 'Cold Comfort Farm – kosher.'

But Clive, like everyone who entered Grandma's aura, fell under her spell – that bewitching knack of making each visitor feel that he or she was the one person she had been longing for. 'Nu, how's it with you?' she'd pat your arm. My Mum visited her every week and sometimes twice. All the daughters-in-law, all the grandchildren, visited often, except of course Moishe, the unmentioned. Eventually, Grandma told me why: he'd run away from Aunt Ethel, married a blonde barmaid, changed his name to Max and bought a Betting Shop.

'Do you miss him, Grandma?'

Grandma went deaf.

On Festivals and High Holy Days, sons with wives, daughters, grandchildren, nephews and nieces, gathered to eat many-coursed meals, cooked by Hannah and served by Grandma, who knew by heart each person's favourite portion of chicken. Everyone came except for Moishe/Max, whom she never mentioned anymore than her dead husband. Surrounded by descendants, she presided beaming over the long, white-clothed table. I imagined I was her favourite grandchild, we all did.

My Dad, ('Blessings on his head,') said Grandma, paid most of her household bills. She persuaded him to part with middling to large amounts of cash to underwrite Cyril's and Nahum's crack-brained schemes; opening fur-shops, selling Army surplus by mail-order, writing a book on hypnosis. 'Such wonderful ideas, they have, my boys,' said Grandma. 'Just a little *mazel*, is all they need,' and she'd pat my father's knee. The fur-shop went bust; Army surplus cluttered the shed and the book gave rise to two law-suits.

Her own generosity became a legend. Whatever you gave her,

she'd say, 'Put it away for later, Bubele.' The gift joined the chocolates, scarves and perfumes piled into a mahogany cupboard. When she grew old, over ninety, she'd forget who'd given what, and give back your own bottle of cologne or box of stale chocolates. Old Jews with wispy beards, wearing fur hats and caftans, came begging to the door and left clutching beribboned boxes and muttering Yiddish blessings. Your pockets would be filled with boiled sweets 'for the journey,' although you weren't going anywhere.

After she became too frail to bake and too purblind to sew, her days were passed in the narrow hall, sitting on a high oak stool beside the open front door, reading Talmud through a magnifying glass, her lips mouthing the Hebrew. My father's brother, the only person I ever knew who didn't admire her, claimed she did it to show off. If true, she spent many hours to impress us, her hands icy cold to touch, her eyes milky-blue.

'Why don't you like Grandma, Uncle Louis?'

'Ask her kids,' came his laconic reply.

Slowly, slowly, the reins of her household slipped her grasp; her zest diminished. A niece did the shopping; a lady was sent in from the Jewish Welfare Board to give her a bath. When granddaughters visited, she'd call them by their mothers' names.

Death came through the unlocked front door in the guise of one of the *yeshiva-bokkers*. Grandma stretched up to pull down a box of biscuits from the present-filled cupboard and suffered a heart attack. Her children, grandchildren and great grandchildren shook their heads: 'Things will never be the same.' And they were right. The family fell apart without its holding centre.

I didn't attend the funeral. I can't quite remember why. I recall that I'd busied myself with some plans for my children. My mother pursed her lips – Moishe and I the only ones missing. They'd sent a telegram but Moishe missed his own mother's funeral! Everyone remarked.

The household at number twenty-seven staggered on for a few years. No one summoned the family together again for a celebration. Aunt Hannah gave away the monster serving dishes and the 20-pint saucepans. What had seemed so well-knitted unravelled so fast.

Could the aunts and uncles have hated one another?

Twenty years on and all her sons have joined her, except Moishe. My Mother believes he lives in America. 'Curses on him!' Ginni never came back.

When number twenty-seven was sold, the grandchildren rushed to grab souvenirs. I bore off a photo. Clive said the ornate frame didn't match our cream settee, so I hung it in the spare bedroom where I don't see it that often. She's about fifty in the picture, that smiling, gentle, olive-skinned old lady, who remained a beauty all her life. I've never forgotten her. None of her children held a candle to her. Now the aunts and uncles are gone – I never give them a thought.

When I remember Grandma, I see her holding my first baby, Berenice, her eleventh great-grandchild. Babies adored her lap. My Dad stands behind, looking happy without his crutches. But another image shadows the first: I see the web that the spider had woven between the lilac branches and the insects trapped within the sticky folds of its thread.

Yiddish Words:
Goyim – non-Jews
Schwarzers – black people
mesuggah – crazy
Nebbich – a pity
latkes – potato pancakes
mazel – luck
Bubele – sweetheart
yeshiva-bokker(s) – student(s) in a Talmudic school

-oOo-

Riding
Round
Eros

W e'd arranged to meet outside the Student Union in Malet Street. That was the winter when I just turned twenty-one and had picked up more philosophy than sense. With my birthday money I'd bought a turquoise blue Vespa. He was late. I was about to drive off, when he appeared, unruffled, smiling. Down Regent Street we rode. Christmas decorations up already, air smelling of mist and petrol. Through my duffel-coat, Hassan's arms squeezed my waist; his extra weight made me wobble. He held me tighter, his breath warming the back of my neck. My God, if Mum could see me – careering round Piccadilly Circus with him attached to my middle! A bloody silly idea meeting at uni, we should've met outside the theatre. This whole thing between Hassan and me, teaching him English culture and all that, wouldn't work. Who was I fooling? English culture! Ha! Hassan didn't give a damn.

Round and round Eros we rode with my hair blowing across his face. I lost my nerve – stuck in the inside lane – not daring to cross the stream of cars to get into Leicester Square. He thought I was doing it on purpose, laughed in my ear and hugged me tighter. On our fourth circuit, a cop flagged me down and asked to see my licence: 'What d'you think you're playing, Miss?'

The play was super; several people walked out in the interval – always a good sign. In the bar, I met two blokes from college. Everyone drank beer and argued over the meaning. No one meant to be unkind but Hassan, poor chap, was left out completely. The play's second half was mindstretchingly incomprehensible.

Hassan whispered, 'Why they stuck in dustbins?'

'Shush,' I replied. I didn't know either.

A minute later I looked at him. He'd fallen asleep (we had standing room at the back of the stalls) with his head tucked into the crook of his elbow, like a sleeping goose. The first three curtain calls didn't wake him. At the fourth, he woke up, shook himself. His teeth glinted; I smelt aftershave. 'The play didn't disturb you, I hope? There's a Tube outside the theatre.'

After that evening, I didn't bother going to the Union canteen. The man was a moron. I'd drop him. After ten days eating in my college canteen, I got bored eating lunch with the same old college crowd. Besides – suppose Hassan really needed my help – perhaps he'd been tired that night. It had been a very difficult play. Oughtn't I to find out about Ghana and Nkrumah and all that?

He was sitting at our usual table – not alone. Since meeting him, I noticed African students more – they weren't all lookalikes. The other two men were lighter coloured and taller. 'This is her.'

Funny, how emphasising one little word makes you special. The theatre incident wasn't mentioned and the friends acted like I was extraordinary. Whatever I said, they laughed. I got wittier and wittier. Then Hassan clicked his fingers. Before I'd realised, they'd vanished. One minute I was playing Queen of the Jungle – the next we were alone.

A silence. It lasted so long I started to wriggle and then he said: 'Will you come to my house?'

'What?'

'Next Tuesday?'

'Yes, yes, I will.' The speed of the reply surprised us both.

On Monday night, I washed my hair in beer. The plaid skirt I'd worn the first time we'd met was back from the cleaners. Would he notice? When I parked in his street, the turquoise-blue Vespa stuck out in its shiny newness. What a slum: gardens full of torn-up of paper; scrawny cats scratching in overflowing dustbins; uncut privet hedges. Suppose someone who knew me saw me? I'd only stay a few minutes. I rang a jangly bell. He took a long time coming. Someone had painted his front door red. We climbed two flights of a wooden staircase. The blue frayed carpet had loose treads.

'They're dangerous. Someone'll fall. Why don't you ask the landlord to fix them?'

No answer.

'You don't have to be scared.'

Still no answer.

'I can ask him for you.'

'Ask him? How can I? This is my house. I am the landlord.'

He owned a whole house! 'What does your father do?'

'He has land.'

'Does he have lots of wives?'

'Some.'

'D'you live in a palace?'

'No, I live here.'

Hassan slept in the smallest of the five rooms and rented out the other four. There wasn't much furniture: a bed; a desk; a bookcase and, taking up the whole of one wall, a spiky-legged radiogram with gold knobs and shiny black veneer. Expensive.

'See that – for taking home.'

I could hardly have missed it. A red woollen dressing gown hung behind the door. I twirled the tassels.

'Don't touch,' said Hassan.

'Alright,' I said and let the tassel drop.

We sat side by side on the single bed, which had a lacy bedspread. I babbled whatever came into my head, the weather, College, books I'd been reading. The room was so narrow that Hassan could stretch across and catch hold of a box of chocolates stuck behind a volume of Wordsworth propped up on the mantelpiece. 'These are yours.'

'Mine?' I'd never seen them before – Cadbury's Roses, the medium-sized box.

'Yes. Yours.'

'Oh, yes, of course. Thanks, thanks very much.' The cellophane wouldn't unwrap. He tried to help. We fumbled. He ripped the top off the box and we sat munching crispy toffees and hazelnut logs. After eating six, I knew I should stop but you know how nerves turns you greedy. I started unwrapping a seventh. Hassan picked the box out of my lap and dropped it onto the carpet. Chocs rolled everywhere. I bent forward to pick them up and his arm swung across my chest like an iron bar. With neither a word nor a kiss, he pushed me backwards against the wall. The room was over-heated from a two-bar electric fire; sweat trickled under my arm-pits. A weak ray of sunlight beamed into my eyes. I squeezed them shut. Easier to keep still. My clothes began sliding off. My tights seemed to roll themselves down. Cloth against cloth became skin against skin. His felt silky. I knew I should get up and I could not move. I peeked through half-shut eyes; he was leaning on one elbow, looking me up and down, down and up. He had not tried to kiss me, nor said a single, bloody word. A giggle surged but before it broke, he grabbed my hand and curled it round his prick. My God! Oh, no! My fingers hardly met. That thing would never fit inside. Black it was all over – the tip as well. That black tip shocked. Pretty silly. Was I expecting a pink one? I tried to sit up but too late, the bloody toffee gagged me. Pinning my arms to my sides, he slid his prick inside. I must've been wet enough for nothing tore. He drove in a few times and came with a grunt: I let tears come. (I've always been able to cry at will.) Pulling himself up to my face, he kissed my eyelids and hair, his mouth so soft.

'At home, little pigeon, we never kiss. This habit is dirty so I kiss only to please you.'

Pleased! I wasn't pleased. I hadn't come; everything had happened too fast. I cried harder. Starkers on a bed, on Tuesday, December the ninth, at twelve-fifteen, instead of being safe in the library with *Principles of History Teaching (2nd edition)*. Not knowing what to do, I carried on until the sobs got sniffly. Should I make a scene? No one had forced me here. I looked for another toffee; they lay scattered – sweet promises out of reach.

By themselves, my fingers found his prick. He knelt and wrapped my legs round his waist, neatly crossing my ankles across his bottom. Slowly, he began to screw – as if there were no clocks and nothing to do except what we were doing. And this time, a full orchestra played an anthem I'd only heard before on a penny whistle. I flew over mountains and rivers and oceans. Time stopped so I don't know how long it lasted. Smells of gas, perfume and spunk. Hassan stretched a towel under my bottom – the bottom sheet was damp.

We slept.

I woke up first, sprawled half-across him, my hair falling over the edge of the bed. So happy he looked with his eyes closed, his hand resting against my thigh, chocolate on cream. Someone had scarred twelve parallel lines down his belly. Limp, his penis looked no larger than anyone else's. I crouched, covering his belly and legs in a tent of hair. My mouth found his tangled groin, moist, warm, smelling of

vanilla. I sucked. The world shrank: hair, mouth, prick. You know that
sonnet: *An expense of spirit in a waste of shame is lust in action.* I've
forgotten how the rest goes. But old Willy had got it ever so wrong.

'On Thursday, what time you be here?'

'The same time.'

That winter's cold never touched me. Tuesday and Thursday
afternoons in Finsbury Park left a glow which heated my whole week.

At home one weekend, Mum said: 'Your skin's clearer. I'm so glad
you've given up smoking. You still seeing Tom?'

Tom? That miserable jerk in a college scarf. 'Oh, no. Not him any
more.'

'Never mind. That'll give you more time for work.'

She didn't know (I wasn't going to tell her) that I hadn't had more
than a C+ all term. I should've done better; I had plenty of time. Hassan
never asked me out. After the theatre fiasco, I didn't ask him. He never
asked what I did when we weren't together. I daydreamed – his thigh,
his smile, his prick – jigsaw pieces which never fitted. What a
suspension of disbelief that we indulged in that Spring – those
afternoons in the over-heated room, never speaking more than a few
words, our love-making growing wilder and wilder. One Tuesday we
started coiled up against the pillows, rolled down the length of the
bed, tipped over the edge and finished up under the desk without ever
coming apart.   Every time I met him, we made love three times,
sometimes four. If I looked at my watch, he'd say: 'Wait ten minutes,
little pigeon, only ten, if you want to fly again.' Smooth as a baby's his
skin, without rough patches on his bottom like we have. We talked
lovers' talk. He never said, 'I love you.' I said it often.

One May afternoon, fluffy pink-eyed clouds scuttered across a
blue sky. We lay side-by-side, touching all the way down our bodies
until my feet stretched six inches beyond his. There'd never be another
winter. In a voice so low I could barely hear, he said his father'd died
and next month he'd return to Ghana. 'My uncle is the new chief. I must
attend the enstoolment.'

Hassan's father had been a Paramount Chief! He crouched on the
carpet to show me how he had to prostrate himself each time they met
– lying flat on his face, his round-cheeked bottom in the air. As soon as
I started to laugh, he stopped. For the first time since I'd known him, he
talked about the constant petty insults he'd suffered in our so-called
civilised country. In his first month, before he learnt to tell white faces
apart, he'd gone to his lodgings, rung the wrong bell and thinking that

the woman who answered had been his landlady, started up the stairs. The woman screamed and called the police. I loved him for telling me. 'This poem – I had to learn in school – you know it...*I wandered lonely on a cloud of daffodils*? I was thinking daffodils were insects, you know – like mosquitoes. You think English people laugh at us?'

'Of course not!' I was lying. We sat cross-legged, facing each other, naked on the narrow bed. Why shouldn't I give up teaching and join him in Africa?

'I'll live with the women, learn your customs and then...' This sacrifice didn't seem to impress. Wouldn't he marry a white woman, I demanded? How could he complain of prejudice and be prejudiced himself?

'But Little pigeon, I am married. I have two wives already.'

Two! Shy, diffident Hassan, who'd asked me which fork to use when he dined in Hall!

'My father sent them to me when I was eighteen. They are bush girls. If I take a white woman – I will send them back to their villages and I shall keep the little boys.'

He had three sons. So what! I could be their step-mother. I could wear a solar-topee and a bush shirt – like Katherine Hepburn. 'D'you live in the jungle, Hassan?'

'No! Jungle is on coast. Savannah is dry.'

I didn't know about savannahs. His father kept fifty Barbary horses and he supposed them still to be there. I swopped the helmet for a jockey cap and galloped off into the desert/banana plantation/forest/scrub, or whatever savannahs were.

'Now go home, little princess. Already it is after four.' He was dismissing me. The casting had gone skew-whiff. I was playing Desdemona to his Othello. Unhooking the red dressing gown down from behind the door, I made passes like a bull-fighter.

'Put that back,' he snapped.

I left. I managed to stay away for a week. Not longer. How I hated shutting that red front door while the sun shone. Hassan never opened a single window and kept the gas-fire blazing. Nothing more said about my going to Africa.

'I 'll never forget you, little pigeon. Never,' he repeated often.

In spite of what we didn't say, our bodies spoke. As the Bible says, we knew one another. If I had still believed in having one, I'd have said Hassan fucked my soul. And yet, were either of us ever honest, really honest, about ourselves?

On the last Tuesday before he was to leave, Hassan said: 'Let's have lunch in the Union canteen.' He had something to show me. This would be the first time that term we'd agreed to meet outside his room. Perhaps he'd changed his mind? Maybe he wasn't leaving? Maybe, maybe, he'd bought me a ticket? At the thought of actually flying off to Africa, my daydreams scarpered but I hauled them back. Of course I was ready to become a princess at the court of Prince Hassan.

On the Monday night I washed my hair. It was raining again; the canteen smelt of wet coats. I'd come full circle. Same place – we'd met. From the doorway, I could see Hassan at our table and he wasn't alone. Two girls sat with him – two white girls – one with her head bent. Somehow I had to squeeze through those packed tables to the other end of the hall; I couldn't move. Knives and forks jangled; voices babbled. I could hear drumming until I realised it was my own heartbeat. Why was everyone staring? I began to push forward, wading through a sea of noise.

Hassan half-stood up and waved and cried: 'Why you so late, Pigeon? Come, sit down.' He started to introduce the girl. There was no need. I'd guessed already. She wasn't pretty but her grey eyes had the longest lashes. 'Jane, my fiancée. Next week we leave for Ghana. We shall be married after the enstoolment.'

Jane! Jane! Jane! How could I have been so stupid! Why hadn't I guessed? All those clues: the red dressing gown I mustn't touch; the fine-toothed comb; the volume of Wordsworth. He'd never asked me out over weekends or evenings. Never wanted me to phone him. He'd had Jane. I'd been tricked! Rage lumped in my chest. How fat she was! Oh, yes, they liked fat women, didn't they? Hassan was always telling me I was too thin. Fatty looked so smug – I felt like throwing up. Of course, she'd been with him last night. Monday. She'd had Monday night and here I sat on Tuesday, my Tuesday, babbling like a half-wit, while Jane and Hassan purred like cream-fed cats. And the other girl, poor thing, what days were hers? Only seven in the week, dammit? Didn't he give himself a night off?

'Hassan. Terribly sorry. Must rush, it's too late for lunch. Goodbye. Goodbye, Jane. I-I hope you'll be happy, terribly happy.'

Jane could afford her gracious nod.

The dark girl scraped back her chair. 'I'd better go, too.'

Hassan smiled; dazzling affection drizzled over us three women. No one said a single word. Jane must've picked up Hassan's habit of useful silences.

In the lift I asked the dark girl: 'How long?'

'T-ten months. Today's my nineteenth birthday... I thought he...' Her handkerchief smothered the rest.

I rode my Vespa back to hall, raindrops imitating tears on my cheek. My African dream – I could give that up. But those afternoons – those afternoons in Finsbury Park – not them. He'd said that we'd meet again. We'd never meet again and I knew it. He'd said: 'I'll never forget you.' And said it lots of times. Bloody liar! It wasn't true. Already, one hour into parting, I knew that I was the one who'd never forget.

Virtual Reality

T he Editor said glumly: 'Something rum's happening up at Honeybeare Hall, Check it out, will you, Harry?' Bill hates giving the Hall any publicity ever since its owner, Osbert Phipps refused a full-page ad. 'I don't need extra publicity,' Osbert had remarked, looking down what he thinks of as his patrician nose.

So Harry had to go. Traffic jam as usual. He arrived at the Hall forty minutes later, sweating through the back of his terylene jacket. The lime avenue beckoned cool and refreshing – not for long. Outside locked gates, he found a police van and two fire engines, and a dozen anxious people looking as if they didn't know what day of week it was. PC Dobbs unlocked the iron gates and waved him through. Harry knew Honeybeare Hall quite well. Ever since Osbert Phipps started the Happening five summers back, he'd written *The Gazette's* annual piece – splendid tourist attraction, great for local business.

This Monday morning, a couple of leather-aproned gardeners were tying-up plants knocked over in Saturday's summer storm. When Harry called 'Hi,' they ignored him. 'Suit yourselves.' He shrugged and strolled on into the kitchens. Ovens were going full blast, aproned maids strewing nasturtium flowers over platters of steaming beef; the chief steward was waiting to lead the procession of dishes into the Great Hall. At the long oak table Osbert Phipps presided, pot-bellied under a canopied chair with his wife Lucinda wearing an elaborate ruff, beside him under a smaller canopied chair.

'Hi, folks!' No answer from anyone. What the Hell was going on?

This was Monday. There wasn't supposed to be any Happening: the pantries, the cellars, the chapel, the stillroom, the kitchens, the dairies, the stables, the smithy are shut. One hundred and fifty volunteers go home on Sunday nights – back to their real lives – back to 9 to 5 if they're lucky and not much else if they're not.

But not today!

Harry looked around for his girl friend, Liz and found her up in the Minstrel's Gallery! She looked gorgeous in a green velvet bodice showing off her tits. Liz was singing, 'O, Mistress mine, where are ye roaming?' Harry stuck two fingers in his mouth and gave their special whistle. No response. 'And come and see your true love's coming...' Liz warbled.

Harry edged behind Osbert's chair and switched on his tape recorder. Osbert's pretend friends and relations were twittering in that fancy Shakespearean English that he teaches them. Harry tapped Sally Hardcastle's shoulder; she lived two floors down in his block. Sally turned to the young man opposite. 'Unbidden guests are often welcomest when they are gone, are they not?' A bit much from Sally who dropped in whenever she felt like a free drink.

Osbert exclaimed: 'I am never so merry as when I hear sweet music. Mark how her voice is soft and low, an excellent thing in a woman.'

Harry flapped a hand in front of Osbert's face. The man never blinked; the so-called 'gentry' were behaving like the maids in the kitchen, as if he, Harry was invisible. Nothing he could do so he left 'em to it.

Outside the gates, scraps of green canvas lay on the ground. He picked one up. It was a strip of the canvas tunnel that had got smashed by the storm. Every summer, Osbert put one up with dates painted in red along one side, 1998... 1900... 1850 . .. 1598... That was his gimmick: tourists handed over their fiver, walked on down the Time Tunnel and, once through, were supposed to be living in 1598. Weekends only of course. But this weekend the Happening hadn't stopped. Why not?

When Harry got back to *The Gazette*, Bill listened to the tape and sniffed: 'Phipp's visitors are dropping off; punters are watching their cash. A publicity stunt – that's all!'

Harry said, 'Something bloody odd's going on.'

Bill avoided eye contact. 'Isn't that gel of yours one of 'em? What did she say?' They both knew that it wasn't only Liz in there.

Harry said gloomily: 'Liz acted like she hadn't seen me.'

Bill said: 'Those volunteers adore Osbert's phoney view of history.' He tried peering down his nose the way Osbert does. It didn't work; his nose was too short. 'Life on a great Tudor estate. Fulfils everyone, don't ye know. Phipps's a pompous ass but you gotta admit the place makes a first class tourist attraction. He researches for months getting details right – like close stools for the gentry and outdoor jakes for the servants.'

'He's a snob,' Harry said. 'Fancies himself Lord of the Manor. Calls it recreating face-to-face society. Everyone knowing each other, knowing their place. Gives 'em security as well as fancy clothes.'

Bill did another of his sniffs. 'Nah! simple play-acting – a money-making gimmick he's trying – nothing else. That's your angle – write it.'

'OK, you're the boss. But there's more. I mean the people that take part... They become obsessed – like Liz.'

Harry keyed in his story. Something still bothered him. 'What Liz never explains is why they choose the roles they do. Gavin's a bank manager. Why should he want to be a blacksmith, or Tom Dugald be a cobbler, when in real life he's a solicitor? Doesn't make sense. People enjoy working with their hands, I suppose, and touching what they've made. Most of 'em like being given orders by a lord. It's a ready made set-up. Wouldn't suit me.' He straightened his tie. 'They accept really filthy jobs. Take Myrtle, who's a chartered accountant – standing barefoot in a stream washing sheets. Doesn't make sense.'

Bill said with a sneer: 'I notice that Mr and Mrs Phipps get to play Lord and Lady every single blooming year. Never been tempted to have a go yourself?'

'You joking! See me giving up home comforts to prance around in tights showing off my balls!' He chewed off a hangnail. 'My Liz throws herself like a maniac into the whole charade – singing bloody madrigals every weekend.'

'Yeah,' said Bill, 'it's all make-believe.'

'Course. It can't be anything else, can it?' Harry said.

The Gazette's Tuesday headline ran: HONEYBEARE HALL WHAT'S HAPPENING? The Tudor impersonators refused to budge and went on playing their roles. They laughed a lot amongst themselves. Life at Honeybeare continued merrily from High table downwards. Osbert Phipps often boasted that ye olde Englande was self-sufficient – seems he was right. They slaughtered a pig and made sausages.

The story mushroomed. By Thursday the nationals had sent

reporters. Radio Four's newsman turned up. A telly crew was expected. Being the only local journalist, the big boys kept buying Harry beers in *The Kynaston Arms* and asking his opinion. 'It's only a publicity stunt,' he kept repeating.

By Saturday, the queue of cars stretched as far as the T-junction. They were taking a fortune at the gate. But whoever you spoke to inside Honeybeare pretended neither to see or hear.

On Sunday, Harry rushed back to the office. 'The Police have decided: the public can't enter.'

'At last,' Bill sighed, 'Authority come to its senses. All over. Out they come.'

At six o'clock, journalists and relatives were queuing at the gates. Harry waited with them but Liz never showed up. No one did! The stupid joke went on. Supper was served in the great hall. Sir Ralph (Osbert in ruff and cloak) ignoring the police's shouted questions, carved the grinning pig's head with a sprig of rosemary in its mouth. Parker, the Chief Superintendent, muttered darkly about terrorist plots. One of the wives waiting outside grew hysterical so the police sent relatives home; they let the television stay. On the Ten O'clock News, the long shot of the courtyard looked like a BBC2 classic serial.

At midnight, the Chief Superintendent inspected the sleeping estate. He let Harry tag along. Lying on a pile of straw in the barn, they found an old woman wrapped in a quilt. Last time Harry'd seen Margery McDonnell, ex-Latin teacher, she'd been looking bored at a school prizegiving. 'Begone, thou evil spirits,' the crone shrieked as their flashlight beamed her awake.

Each time Harry found Liz, she wouldn't talk. And she'd quite a pong; they all did.

Then the Chief Superintendent's wife, a born-again Christian, recognised Satan's work and suggested the Reverend Augustus ffrench-Crittenden, a specialist in exorcism. His Reverence marched around the Great Hall swinging an incense burner and chanting in Latin. Osbert Phipps, set in his role of Sir Ralph, waved his arms, shouting: 'Will no one rid me of this pesky priest?'

By the second weekend, in spite of no one being allowed in, such crowds turned up that the Police erected crash barriers. In the pub, Harry told the newsmen: 'It's easy to hold back a crowd but how will they deal with 'em inside – wandering around – not breaking any law and having a whale of a time?'

'Experts – that's what we need,' insisted the Police Superintendent and sent for the County Health Officer and a retired psychiatrist. The County Health Officer promised a report and that was the last anyone saw of him. Doctor Stefan Stuffengruber waddled in, spent an hour and waddled out: 'Ze inmates are suffering vrom group hypnosis mit delusions brought about by zere leader. Zey vill only see us ven ve interfere. Also, zey are vey vey 'eppy wiz zat life.'

Week Three began with no one, expert or not, having any ideas on how to stop the Happening happening.

'Let him keep his little joke ticking over until one of them needs an appendix op,' said Bill, gloating over The Gazette's inflated circulation. Harry had his hair cut; the Nine O'clock News were going to interview him.

The deadlock appeared unbreakable, until Bill Izard drove up one evening with nine-year old Tracey in the back seat. Through the iron gates the onlookers watched Bill's wife Marilyn rattling her tambourine, while Ronnie Caulfield, dressed as Tomas, the gypsy king, stomped and olé-ed around her.

Bill snarled: 'What's that oaf Ronnie Caulfield doing with my wife?'

Ronnie's wife, a bun-shaped woman, snarled back: 'What's your wife think she's doin' with my 'usband?'

The two gypsies strolled out of sight arm-in-arm; the gypsy queen's head resting on Tomas' shoulder.

Tracey popped her bubblegum and remarked in an off-hand way: 'Mum can't come back 'cos the tunnel's blown down.'

The surrounding grown-ups gave embarrassed titters. Voices muttered: 'Why not?' 'Out of the mouths of babes . ..' 'What we got to lose...?' 'Let's give it a go.'

After two days wrangling over which department should repair the tunnel, Parks & Open Spaces did. They painted huge red arrows leading to 1998. The Time Tunnel was pegged into place; now Osbert and friends had to be 'persuaded' to come through. The Police kept out the public but let in Press and TV. Five ambulances were on hand; an enterprising Burger van sold cups of tea to weepy relatives.

In the forecourt, family and household servants clustered in a semi-circle around Sir Ralph; two children sheltered under his blue velvet cloak. Beyond the low wall which separated house and grounds, estate folk huddled in separate groups. A dwarf turned cartwheels – with no one clapping he soon stopped.

Stuffengruber, the psychiatrist, hurried onto the forecourt and grabbed Osbert's arm. Osbert, a magnificent Sir Ralph, bent down and shook him off; 'Get thee away, thou pippikin.'

The psychiatrist stumbled onto all fours; the police sergeant rat-tatted into his walkie-talkie and two men in white coats, who must have been hiding behind the lavender hedge, popped up. One rolled back Sir Ralph's sleeve and the other pumped a syringe into his arm. The drug took hold in seconds. The Lord of the Manor swayed back and forth, and sideways, rocking on his heels; his feathered felt hat rolled to the ground. The white coats each seized an elbow. As they reached the tunnel's mouth, the magnate sank to his knees. They hoisted him up. The instant his draggling toes touched the coconut matting, his household gave a collective gasp. In ones and twos they began to trickle after. Osbert Phipps (or was it Sir Ralph?) staggered forwards, brushing aside the held-out microphones.

Cheering broke out, people pushing against one another, grabbing relations. Some came out of the tunnel, laughing, tossing off hats and untying aprons; others hung back and wept. Marilyn Izard, her long hair streaming across her face, clutched her little girl, her black eyes following Tomas, a gypsy king fast materialising into Ronnie Caulfield, one arm over his head as his wife hauled him into her car.

Harry couldn't see Liz in the crowd. Where was she? Forgetting his story, his deadline, he dashed through the tunnel. Hell, he wanted her back. He muttered: 'I'll be more understanding. I'll go Green for her. I'll even recycle plastic bags....'

The forecourt was empty. Scattered on the ground lay spindles of wool, a half-sewn slipper, a posy of fresh herbs, a tambourine trailing red and yellow ribbons.

The Happening was over. But was it?

At last he found her – milking in the cow shed with some seven others, still in Tudor costumes.

'Make haste, Mistress Liza,' said Margery McDonnell, 'There is much to do before the others return.'

Liz said sadly, 'I doubt that they will come.' Warm milk spurted into the bucket. A few drops spattered Harry's brand new trousers. Lucinda Phipps smiled at him. Oh, no, she smiled right *through* him.

'Liz, Liz,' he yelled, 'stop this damfoolery. Come back. Come back to real life!'

He could've grabbed her but he didn't; she wanted to be where she was in that make-believe world. Only the dresses and jerkins were not fancy costumes any longer; they looked like ordinary clothes.

A smell of lavender and thyme wafted across from the herb garden and mingled with the smell of fresh milk. As Harry walked towards the Time tunnel, he glanced backwards at the cow shed, which was growing smaller and smaller. Honeybeare Hall's diamond-paned windows were winking. And with each bewildered step that took him back to the rushed and anxious present, he saw that his smart, cream silk suit was becoming more and more like a costume.

-oOo-

What Big Eyes, Grandma?

Trying her hardest to keep Natalie both amused and quiet, Helen peeps through gaps between her splayed fingers and whispers: 'Where's baby? There she is.'

Natalie, unafraid of Grandma's big, yellow teeth, catches on to the game and spreads podgy little fingers across her face. After six goes, Helen's had enough but Natalie won't stop and Helen sniffs; Sam knew hundreds of games at that age. But what can you expect – both parents working and the child plonked in the crÈche from 8 a.m. to 6 p.m.?

Natalie's soft baby voice says: 'Core. Core. Toe. Toe. Toe.' What the hell does the child want? 'Core. Core. Toe. Toe. Toe.' Natalie can't understand why doesn't Grandma react. Tears well in the corners of her eyes.

The penny drops. Of course: *'Encore – gateaux.'* Biscuits – she wants more biscuits. Helen rummages in an overflowing drawer and rips open a packet of pretzels.

Clutching shiny, brown sticks in chubby fist, the toddler ups her arms to be lifted into her high chair. Helen supposes she'd better remake the Put-u-Up but the mechanism turns spiteful and every time she raises the back, the front swings down. There's a trick to it that Helen can't work out. She'll have to wait for Sam. Now Natalie wants to get down. Natalie wants something else. She waves her arms and jumbles up a mixture of incomprehensible syllables in French and English.

'I'm not really stupid, Precious. Show me what you want.'

Natalie grabs at a book. The over-crammed bookshelf avalanches onto the carpet. What a mess: large and small books muddled up; magazines stacked out of order with pages ripped out. Helen starts picking up loose pages, tut-tutting as she does so. Natalie whimpers; Helen lifts her out of the high chair and gently pulls her thumb out of her mouth. Natalie puts it straight back. She's had more than enough of Grandma and positions herself in front of her parents' closed door, scratching like a kitten at the shiny white wood with her free hand. It's Sunday morning; presumably Sam wants a lie-in. And doesn't he need it! Helen turns the door knob. Natalie pushes through her legs and burrows into the hollow between her parents. Sam has his arm around Marie-Thérèse, whose blonde hair fans across the pillow and covers his right shoulder. Her face is like a flower, eyes for pistils and nose for stamen. They're both asleep; they're both naked; they both look about fifteen. Natalie in her Snoopy pyjamas, bulked out with nappies, doesn't match.

Marie-Thérèse wakes up and, instantly alert, draws Natalie into a magic circle of mother/baby from which Helen is naturally excluded.

Helen has an urge to complain about the loose mattress spring on the Put-u-Up which dug into the small of her back last night but Marie-Thérèse's English wouldn't be up to it. Nor would she or Sam be interested to hear about her dream. She'd like to share and dissipate its menace but it's been a long time since anyone was interested enough to listen – let alone interpret – her dreams.

Sam grunts and buries his head under the pillow. He got up twice last night. Helen heard him comforting Natalie but she never heard Marie-Thérèse. They demand the lot – today's young women: career, husband, child! Imagine Robert getting up for one of her babies. Once, years ago, she asked him to put on a nappy; he pinned it on back to front. Natalie wears paper nappies of which Helen does not approve. They cause nappy rashes; they are not healthy. Closing the bedroom door with an emphatic click, she pads back to the living room. A cigarette is what she needs but smoking isn't allowed; Natalie mustn't passive smoke. She winds up the metal shutters to see what sort of day Paris has on offer. A pale lemon sun edges out behind the blank-eyed apartment block opposite. Nearby factory chimneys are smoking – lucky things! What difference would her one ciggie make with all that pollution! Will Marie-Thérèse let her take Natalie outside? The child never gets enough fresh air. Sunk into the purple Ikea armchair, Helen taps her foot, disgusted varicose veins writhing like blue worms round her calves. A tightening lump in her chest heralds a panic attack – one that she mustn't have – not in front of them. How can she stop the walls bulging in and out, the floor heaving, the ceiling pressing down, the rubber plant panting for water? Find the baby – where is she? With a baby in your arms you can breathe easy.

She finds Marie-Thérèse with Natalie balanced on one hip, stirring a gooey paste for the child's breakfast.

Helen holds out her arms, 'Have you changed her? There's a smell of poo.'

'Tea or coffee?' replies Marie-Thérèse, speaking between clenched teeth.

'Tea, please.' And Helen mutters, 'There is a smell of poo.'

Marie-Thérèse stays silent – she often does. But a few minutes later, she emerges from Natalie's bedroom carrying two rolled-up disposables. 'You ar-re right, Helen. See, Sam 'asn't thrown zese away.'

Justified but anxious, lest Marie-Thérèse toss the nappies into the already overflowing kitchen bin (why is Marie-Thérèse so sluttish?) Helen says eagerly: 'Here, let me... '

The rubbish chute is down the hall. You must be quick before the minute switch goes out and you're left in the dark clutching your smelly bag. Helen clangs the metal lid and jumps back from the whoosh of rancid air. Where does it go – all that rubbish? Bag after bag, chute after chute.

They sit down for coffee and toast, prepared by Sam. 'So what shall we do today – your last day?' Sam's conciliating brown eyes swivel from mother to wife. Marie-Thérèse offers no suggestions. Working a five and a half-day week in a busy solicitor's office, weekends, she prefers to stay home. And she's unbothered to watch Sam clean up the flat. Apart from Marie-Thérèse's law books, nothing is neatly arranged. Helen aches to rearrange expensive wedding presents crammed just anywhere. That lovely red Venetian bowl from Aunt Harriet is being used as an overflow for bills and envelopes. Neither of them appreciate nice things. She'd intended to buy her daughter-in-law a present in the Duty Free but the choice was appalling. She had considered a box of crystallised fruits then couldn't bring herself to pay £13 99p for 500 grams. In the end she bought nothing – even choosing perfume for Marie-Thérèse was too difficult. Such peculiar taste. Fancy decorating Natalie's wall with a poster of Guernica. Picasso's wide screaming faces will give the child nightmares. But when Helen remarks on this Marie-Thérèse merely smiles.

'What about the Monet exhibition?' suggests Sam.

How thoughtful! Sam has remembered his Ma has always adored the Impressionists. 'I'll treat us,' cries Helen.

'Absolutement non.' Marie-Thérèse's voice holds the authority of the magistrate which she will doubtless one day become. 'Too many crowds 'eze not good for Natalie.'

'Natalie can sit on her Daddy's shoulders, can't she?' Helen remembers Sam doing just that nearly thirty years ago. 'Children love outings, don't they?' Arguing with Marie-Thérèse is impossible – the flower-like face closes. At this moment Sam should intervene and show some spirit. But Sam chooses to remake Helen's bed into a couch and then sit at the far end with his face hidden in *The Guardian Weekly*. Although Helen took out a year's subscription to keep him in touch with 'home,' Sam only reads the Sports Pages and the Financial Report.

'Shall I take Natalie for a walk?'

'It's rather chilly,' says Sam.

'How do you know? You haven't been out.'

Marie-Thérèse, trying to make Natalie eat more compote de pommes, which Natalie is spitting out, blobs of compote everywhere, says, to Helen's surprise – why not. Both parents pile layer after layer of bright clothing onto the child.

'She doesn't need a hat and a scarf,' protests Helen.

"Old Grandma's 'and,' snaps Marie-Thérèse.

'I shan't lose her,' says Helen. 'Oh, Sam, we went to the Picasso at the Tate when you were three and you vanished. What a hullabaloo! We found you unrolling toilet rolls in the Ladies.' The young parents don't join in her laughter.

"Old Grandma's 'and tight,' repeats Marie-Thérèse.

'I have had three children, you know,' says Helen defiantly. But not brought up three, has she? No, she has only given birth to three. Let's not think about dead babies. Not today. No Baby Alarms in those days. On her little back Helen had found her – choked in her own vomit. She and Robert had stood two feet apart at the funeral. They did not hold hands. The graves were so tiny; it could have been a pet cemetery. When they got home, they came no closer and silences flourished like weeds in the pretty little house. Helen takes the swaddled child by the arm and marches out. The closing door chops off a gush of high-pitched French, *'Ta Maman est impossible!'*

*

Out of frozen ground, mutilated roses raise crucified arms; the sickly sun has barely cracked ice in the puddles. Pots of dead geraniums fringe balcony rails. Natalie prises up a long splinter of ice and jumps up and down. She loves the ping as the ice shatters. Helen watches, her hands freezing. Unzipping her anorak pocket, she thrusts them inside. Close to, the spikey grass is spattered with dog turds, cigarette stubs and broken beer bottles. People are so dirty! A hot flush is creeping up her neck and spreading across her shoulders; her eyes unfocus. Why does no one tell you how trivial life becomes at fifty? And it wasn't so hot at forty either. That was the year Sam left for Durham and Robert started staying late at the office. What a cliché – that wishy-washy Caroline. At least that caper's over. She swings Natalie onto her lap but Natalie struggles and doesn't want Grandma's cold lips against her warm cheek. It's not the same, is it? Not like it used to be with Sam and Margaret. Where is Margaret now? Last time they'd met, Meg had hissed some impossible things. Meg and the little last one. The lost one. Helen pushes such thoughts aside. How much younger was that baby than Natalie is now – six months? Each breath Natalie draws pushes Helen closer towards the unthinkable. No, it wasn't like this with her own.

She leans on the railings above the throughway watching Sunday cars zoom ten metres beneath. On the other side of the road the tree-lined Seine flows slowly. An emerald green barge with a rowboat and two bicycles strapped to the stern, trundles up river, check curtains in its windows flapping in the breeze. A black-haired woman about Helen's age opens the cabin door, laughing over her shoulder at someone inside. I'd love to be on a barge, thinks Helen, and then realises that she's not been watching Natalie, who's sat down on the wet grass. 'Oh, Natalie!' Helen drags her away and attempts brushing off sticky mud. Natalie starts to fidget. 'Come on, Natalie. Where's baby? Where's BABY?' Natalie won't play. Helen points to the boat. 'See the boat?' Natalie can't see high enough. Helen jumps her up onto the railings. Natalie wants to walk along the edge. The boat is almost out of sight. Helen holds her hand and keeps the other arm around her legs. Natalie is screaming, half-fearful, half-excited. Helen, wanting to see more of black-haired woman on the boat, drags her along. The railings are slippery with melted frost and greasy, too. Helen's hot flush has reached her thighs. She must get back. She hauls Natalie down. 'Core, core,' the child shouts.

Helen jumps her up again. Natalie stands taller than Grandma, high as the sun above the chimneys. Her woolly red hat blocks out the sun. She has turned into a giant. Helen's chest tightens, her breathing shortens. Helen, panting, lets go of Natalie's hand. 'Big girl, Natalie.' Natalie shouts for joy. Natalie's feet in their tight red boots slide forward, Natalie's body tips backwards and topples to the ground ten metres below. If that happened, would she have time to cry, 'Ma-ma, Ma-ma'? The sound the body makes as it collides against the concrete is Splat! Just like the comics Sam used to read. Natalie would lie quite still with her head turned to one side, the cold air spreading a pretty pink over her cheeks.

That could never happen – it would be too terrible!

Helen clutches Natalie's legs and drags her off the railings. She hears herself panting: 'I've got to stop this.' Natalie wriggles in her arms to climb back. 'Core, core.' Her little boots are digging into Helen's stomach.

'Alright,' says Helen. Natalie's face is new and young with nothing written there. Nothing ever will be. 'Suppose we both do.'

The feeble sun has given up; it feels bitterly cold. With icy hands Helen lifts Natalie until the excited child is clinging round her neck, Helen clambers up herself, swaying to get her balance. The scene replays – Natalie on the railing in her tight red boots and Helen's right arm around her legs. Nothing bad has ever happened to Natalie. Nothing bad ever shall. 'I've been through the whole damn lot, my Precious. You won't be missing much.' As Helen's left leg slides along the parapet, the gusset of her tights rips. Her last pair – so what? Natalie's soft hand lies warm in Helen's. Helen fills her lungs with cold, cold air. They leap from the parapet hand in hand. The wind floats them forward and upward as they swoop out towards the Seine, Natalie's coat inflates like a balloon. The barge is sailing upstream – the black-haired woman waving frantically at them, her mouth gaping. But Helen and Natalie never reach the water; they drop. Natalie lets go of her hand. The screaming woman from Picasso's *Guernica* swims up from the pavement. The concrete slaps Helen's face with a long-imagined thud. Aah!

Back at the apartment Sam has finished hoovering. 'Nice walk, Ma?' The place looks much tidier already. Good boy, he must have aired the room. How fresh it smells!

'I asked you if you had a nice walk?'

What can she say? Marie-Therèse, looking like a toreador in black tights and an scarlet jacket, picks up Natalie's mud-spattered coat with two fingers, sniffs and drops it into the laundry basket. Helen is waiting for the comment; it doesn't come. And then Marie-Therèse says: 'We shall try the Monet, I zink, since you want to so much.'

Helen says: 'Oh, I do. I do.' Natalie toddles across the carpet, puts her Snoopy into Grandma's arms and leans against her knees. Her flush fades; her shivering stops.

'And *merci* for the walk.' Marie-Therèse offers her daffodil smile.

'Oh, think nothing of it,' says Helen. 'Nothing of it.'

Sam rolls up the Hoover cord and arranges it in the cupboard. Passing behind his wife, he pinches her bottom. His smile includes his mother. 'Having a good time, Ma? Enjoying yourself?'

Helen says: 'Oh, yes, yes.' Natalie's cheek is so warm to kiss. 'Where's the baby? There she is.'

And family life goes on...

-oOo-

Love in the Time of...

M acrinus knows himself to be ugly, knows himself to be rich. The family domain covers one half of the valley of the Wive and half a hill beyond. Should not forty slaves and six vineyards and one water mill, set a counterweight to his bandy legs, barrel chest and dangling arms?

Apparently not.

Lucrece has refused him twice, in spite of twelve capons given to her father; in spite of a bolt of Chinese silk with sunbeams trapped in its shimmering folds, in spite of the common boundary they share along the river bank.

He creeps after her; he seizes every pretext to visit Paulus, his neighbour, in the hope of catching a glimpse of his daughter. She plays beneath the apple trees and lets the falling blossom freckle her face and neck. She likes fishing for trout in the stream which runs under willows behind the orchard. He lies hidden in long grass, watching from the opposite bank. Her temper is unsteady; if she does not catch any fish, she beats the little slave-girl with her rod, then repents, kisses the girl and gives her almonds. Whatever Lucrece does, Macrinus finds no fault. But his days of spying are numbered, like Persephone she is soon to be shut away. Once her fourteenth birthday passes, her days are spent in the women's quarters, Paulus judges her too old to linger in the market, joking with the fish-sellers, too old to roam the meadows.

Macrinus, although he visits Paulus at every opportunity, can no longer catch those casual glimpses that fuelled his love.

One day he visits Paulus and brings up the subject dear to his heart. 'Are you seeking to find a husband for Lucrece?'

'Have you anyone in mind?' replies Paulus. And to his chagrin Macrinus realises that his neighbour cannot conceive of him being a suitor. For three months, although he takes daily walks along the two properties' common boundary, he does not meet her. He must wait until August, where (in the stadium that his money has helped to build) the annual games in honour of the Emperor Trajan will be held. There, amongst a bevy of shawled and veiled landowners' women, she scatters rose petals onto the shoulders and head of a blonde-bearded barbarian, who has won both discus and javelin. Aelfled is his name. What else could Macrinus expect?

He sits alone in the round tower room, above the tops of oak and pine trees. Herons' eyes gleam from the mosaic floor. The artist has set foxes and rabbits, hares and hounds circling in a perpetual chase. Macrinus has forbidden representations of any human form. He rubs his slate clean, refills the space with shapely symbols. The poems express the love in his heart. They have one subject, one object. Her name is never written; her essence fills each poem like the scent of narcissus, the song of the skylark, the softness of goose-down. His Greek is tolerable, his Latin excellent. And the simple fact of being ugly rules his life; just as the simple fact of being lovely rules hers.

So what can he do, when Aelfled, victor of the games, begs his aid? Aelfled woos but lacks words elegant enough to match his handsome face. What else can such an ugly, rich cripple do but offer the lovesick warrior the use of a poem and then another and then another? Not since polio withered his left leg at nine, has Macrinus felt such a griping in his guts as each poem passes from his hand to Aelfled's. Nightly he suffers; daily he scowls and lets the fair-haired giant copy another stanza. Aelfred's great hand claps him on the shoulders: 'A man could cross seven oceans before finding such a friend. She loves them so; she can't get enough of them.'

At the wedding, Macrinus smiles and smiles until his neck muscles cramp with tension. The garlanded guests drink wine by the flagonful. He wishes that it would choke them and knows that it will not for it is excellent wine from his own vineyards. Aelfled carries the virgin bride to the rose-filled upper chamber, while the guests, sprawled on couches, make ribald allusions to untying knots and cocks and

Macrinus' love scratches like a fishbone in his jealous gullet.

Not for long, however. The marriage lasts less than six months. Macrinus attends Aelfled's funeral. The young hero has succumbed to smallpox and childless Lucrece retires to a newly-established nunnery. Macrinus tries to see her before she leaves. The servant will not allow him into her apartments. His letters remain unanswered. He supposes that she is overcome with grief. Paulus, bent and aged after her departure, complains: 'A bride of the Nazerene is no daughter of mine.'

The nunnery is built in the hills behind a rammed earth wall. Such foundations are becoming fashionable as conditions worsen and the barbarians fan further inland burning and pillaging these outposts of threatened empire. Macrinus, having armed his field slaves and safe behind his pine-clad hills, feels secure.

Each June on the anniversary of her enclosure, he saddles his mule and rides twelve miles to Saint Severine, where Lucrece, now Sister Aelfleda, offers him honey cakes. Facing one another in a small, white-washed room, he holds out a goblet but she will never raise her veil to sip the Falerian wine Macrinus has imported from Rome.

Every year, as he rises to say farewell, he proposes she end her widowhood. As seasons pass and the surrounding countryside grows more devastated and barbarian raids increase in number and severity, his hopes rise in proportion. Surely she will forget her girlhood passion and return such steadfast faith, friendship and devotion? Blood must cool with time! It seems not so. Her response never varies. Gently she says, 'No, Macrinus, no. I can never give you what you want.'

Each year, the same ritual, the visit rises to its crescendo – his proposal – then diminishes – her quiet refusal. The time spent in the white-washed room lasts less than one, and more than half an hour – these meagre minutes are all he has to cherish for twelve months. On the twenty-fifth occasion she remarks: 'Do you know today is my birthday?'

He blushes. He does not know; has never known. What has he known of her – this veiled, unchanging figure who remains the fourteen year-old mistress of his dreams? Now that he knows his visit falls on her birthday, on each occasion, he offers a gift, a pottery jar, a knife, a bay tree, which gravely she accepts before handing it over to the abbess.

On her fiftieth birthday – he asks the annual question and can not forbear to add: 'Soon it will be too late, Lucrece. I am sixty-seven years old.'

'The years have been more than kind to you,' says the nun. Perhaps she means that age has weathered his ugliness. The withered leg so heinous in youth is hardly noticeable in the elderly man.

'I shall not ask you again,' says Macrinus, who feels the weight of useless years gather behind his back, pushing him towards eternity.

'I shall not ask again,' he repeats. 'I have worshipped you all my life. This is the last time.' The jealous anger he once felt rekindles in his breast. 'You have been – and you are – foolish to despise such a love.'

She is silent. Then, to Macrinus' astonishment, she laughs and with one swift movement, rises from the wooden stool. The laugh ends on a gentlest of sighs. 'Have you known what you have loved?'

'Of course. I can recall every feature of your face.'

Turning her back, she begins freeing head and shoulders from the veil. Her black hair, which once fell below her waist, is cut short and speckled with grey, her neck as curving as a swan's. Slowly she turns. Macrinus can barely manage to keep his gaze on hers – her face so ravaged by the pox. Striated skin writhes around the craters of her pitted cheeks. The sight is monstrous!

Macrinus bites his lip so hard that it will be bruised for weeks.

The room faces west. Through the narrow aperture late afternoon sun lights up the ruined face. 'Before he died Aelfled told me who had written the poems that won me.' She pauses and asks without a trace of mockery in her black, unaltered eyes, 'And you'd have married me thus? It was better, my friend, that you kept your dreams. Mine were lost long ago.'

He grabs the veil and hands it to her. Smashes the wine pitcher onto the flagstones and, as he limps away, stamps onto fragments of pottery. He never returns. In his will, he donates money for the upkeep of Saint Severine and its enclosed sisters. He leaves careful instructions for his burial.

Seventeen hundred years after the last Roman left, workmen laying a fibre optic cable beneath the town's oldest street dug up a marble chest containing human bones. When the archaeologists had finished sorting the bones, they assembled two skeletons; one belonging to an old woman and another – a male with a twisted spine and shortened leg.

-oOo-

*IRON Press
publishes the most
interesting new
writing from its
own region (The
North-East), the
rest of the UK,
and the world.
Send for our book
list pronto! Our
address is on page
two.*

*